KAREN'S WAY

AARON H. FOSTER

Aaron H. Foster

Copyright © 2015 Aaron H. Foster

Fulton Books, Inc.
Meadville, PA

First originally published by Fulton Books 2015

ISBN 978-1-63338-081-3 (paperback)
ISBN 978-1-63338-082-0 (digital)

Printed in the United States of America

CHAPTER 1

"Let's pick up the refrain on line 26 in 'Smoke Gets in Your Eyes.' Also, sopranos, hold those last notes just a bit longer," the music teacher requested, holding up her baton. This choir class was especially enjoyed by Karen Spanek, a senior at Stanton High, a city of seventy thousand.

The choir finished the song, ending with the three o'clock bell ringing. This was Karen's final class of the day.

"Karen, I need to see you after class," Mrs. Finley, her music teacher, declared. The thirty-eight-member choir broke up with students in various size groups leaving the room. Karen joined Mrs. Finley who was scanning some sheet music she had on her desk. "I was going to ask you to sing the solo part of our second song," Mrs. Finley said as she smiled up at Karen.

"Yes, I can do it because I have looked over the music and practiced it two times." Karen answered.

"Thank you, Karen, you have a beautiful, clear voice," Mrs. Finley replied. "The choir has been asked to sing at the auditorium in the spring festival."

"I must run, Mrs. Finley, I have to go to work later," Karen stated.

Karen left hurriedly, carrying a backpack full of books. Edna Finley was pleased with Karen.

However did Karen make such high marks atone as she always was? Edna thought.

The halls were nearly empty as she made one more stop at Mrs. Trasko's English class. She looked up as Karen entered.

"How may I help you?" she asked.

"Would you help me with my speech I'm giving in my speech class?"

"I'm happy to help," Mrs. Trasko answered. She read through the typed speech Karen handed her. Her speech was well written and prepared. "It's nicely done and well-thought-out." She wished her good luck.

Karen thanked her and left.

One of the best English students we have ever had, Mildred Trasko thought, *and such a joy to teach. But Karen always appeared to be lonely and self-driven toward excellence and very intelligent.*

Karen continued on outside to a nearby corner to wait for a city bus. A group of her girl classmates passed by in a car, stopping for the traffic light. The driver asked Karen if she would like a lift somewhere. Karen declined the offer. She was dressed in jeans and slightly worn blouse. Karen shifted the heavy backpack at her feet. She was always neat, with only a slight amount of makeup.

Five foot three with auburn hair, deep blue eyes, and a light complexion set on a model's face gave her the classic look. Her resolve was that an excellent education would get her out of her recent situation. Karen's mother was never there for her during all this time of growing up. Ruth Spanek's week revolved around the weekend of drinking beer and playing bingo around her part of town.

Ruth Spanek, Karen's mother was in her early forties, with dark hair and better-than-average looks that had been neglected over the past few years. Her constant smoking and drinking wasn't helping any in this department.

Karen's normal week was a grueling one. She was a straight A student in high school. Three nights a week, she works in a busy local restaurant. Then she walks a few blocks home and studies until midnight.

The typewriter she used was an older electric model IBM. It cost her sixty dollars of low wages that she had saved up. A computer was out of the question.

A city bus pulled up, opening its doors. Ed Highsmith greeted her. She took a seat behind him.

"How is high school coming along, Karen?"

"I'm still making straight As, Mr. Highsmith."

He was one of the few who appeared interested in her. Ed thought she was always alone, worked hard, and studied so hard.

What parents wouldn't be proud of her? Somehow, she had some inner purpose going for her, he surmised.

It was late afternoon as the bus arrived on the north side of Stanton. The houses were less cared for and run-down. They passed by houses having broken down cars sitting in front of them. Karen got off at the next corner. Her neighbor Molly Holland was out front to greet her.

"Hi, sweetie, you doing all right?" Molly asked.

"Hi, Molly, I'm tired. Wish I didn't have to go to work tonight," Karen replied. She was due at the restaurant at six o'clock, in uniform. She walked up to a small three-bedroom house that needed painting.

Going inside, she went into her room and dumped her backpack. The room was brightly painted, with curtains at the windows. Karen had done all the work by herself.

Her mother's room was a wreck. The bed was unmade, dresses lying over chairs with ashtrays full of cigarette butts.

Karen glanced at the clock and began to do some household chores. Then she took a shower and changed into a waitress uniform. After combing her hair, she left for work, seven blocks away. Before leaving, she left a short note on the kitchen table.

She was greeted by Molly as she walked out front.

"I'm going to the thrift store in the morning. Do you want to go along?"

"Sure do, I'll be over," Karen answered.

Molly Holland was more like a mother to her than her own mother, Karen decided. It was just starting to get dark as she walked to work.

Minutes later, she arrived at Brown's Restaurant, where she was greeted by everyone. The restaurant was packed with middle-class patrons. The menu had a nice variety, and the food was well prepared.

The evening wore on with Karen busily waiting tables. The tips she received totaled seven dollars and fifty cents. By nine thirty, the last customer had left.

The tables were set for Saturday. Mr. Brown gave Karen her check, thanking her for her work.

How many teenagers would work as hard as this one does? he thought as he let her out the front door. *That one will surely go places someday.*

Karen walked home slowly, tired beyond measure. She finally arrived home and let herself in, after unlocking the door. She went into the kitchen and sat down at the table. Her mother evidently was still at the Friday night bingo parlor.

She then went into her room and changed into a nightgown. Then she studied and typed some school papers until eleven thirty and went to bed. She fell into a deep sleep, after the many hours of her day.

The bed creaked with someone on it. It was her mother, saying, "Just wanted to say good night, love." A slight tinge of alcohol filled the room. Half awake, Karen knew it was her mother.

"Hi, Mom," she replied. "How was your day?" Karen questioned.

"It was the same old thing. Worked all day on the production line," her mother said. "Do you want anything to eat, honey?" Ruth asked.

"I ate while on break at Brown's, Mom."

"I'm not much of a mom to you, sweetie, but I love you," her mother said blankly as she left the room. Karen could hear the water running in the bathroom as her mother brushed her teeth.

What had caused her mother to just give up on life? Karen pondered. Perhaps it was after the death of her father when Karen was seven years old.

This appeared to be a turning point in her mother's attitude about her life in general.

Saturday, Karen slept late, awakened by freshly brewed coffee. She put on a housecoat and went into the kitchen. Her mother was reading the morning paper, smoke curled up from a cigarette in the ashtray.

"Good morning, daughter, let me cook you some breakfast," her mother remarked.

"Sounds good to me, Mom. I get tired of eating cereal after awhile."

Her mother quickly had bacon, eggs over easy, toast, with hash browns set in front of her.

"They are having a drawing at Bill's bar tonight, so I thought at least I would fix you something this morning," Ruth said. "You doing all right in school?"

"My grade average is 4.0 so far this year," Karen answered, looking for a hint of praise.

Her mother generally signed her report card, never commenting on it. She could at least give some hope or praise, Karen wished. She ate breakfast in silence, not making any comments, lost in thought.

After breakfast was over, her mother began to clean and straighten up the house. She even hung up her clothes and made her bed.

What had gotten into her? Karen questioned. So unlike her mother. Karen made her own bed and dressed for the day. Around ten o'clock, there was a knock on the door.

It was Molly waiting for Karen to join her. She went outside, and they left in Molly's '72 Pontiac. They chatted while driving and soon parked at a building marked simply "Thrifty."

"Can I get you something you need?" Molly asked.

"No, not now, but I would like a new dress for graduation," Karen answered.

Molly was more than just a wonderful neighbor; she was a true friend. Many times, this kindly woman was the only one she could turn to for advice and friendship. Molly was an excellent seamstress, always ready to help Karen with any sewing need. Molly's house was the one place she could go to for love and understanding.

They went inside the well-kept store. Customers were just beginning to filter in, looking for a bargain. They both enjoyed each other's company. Each would ask the other about different pieces of clothing that looked to have color and style. The choices Karen made would help her make it through the winter.

Paying for their purchases, they went outside and got into Molly's car. Before starting the car, Molly said, "Sweetie, if you ever need me, call me anytime because you are like my own."

Karen reached over and hugged this little woman who had helped her so many times before. "Molly, you will always be like a kin to me," Karen said, smiling at her.

"Let's go to my house and look at some dress patterns that would look good on you, honey." She than backed out of the parking place and headed for home. Later, they drove into Molly's driveway.

Molly unlocked her front door, and they went inside. The house was always well kept and clean. They both sipped iced tea as they leafed through a pattern book that Molly had brought out. Both agreed on one dress in particular.

"No one in town will look this nice," Molly said, tapping her finger on it. It will be my graduation present to you, love. I'm the best seamstress in town," she said, smiling. "What's going to happen after high school, Karen?"

"I'm going to get a college education and leave this town. The only person I'll really miss is you, Molly," Karen stated. "I must do some studying before I go to work at Brown's tonight." She left, thanking Molly for the ride. Going inside, her mother had done some more housework.

She had been working on her hair and nails. An outfit was hanging in the doorway to her mother's bedroom. Obviously, it was to be worn that evening. It had been freshly washed and ironed. Her mother greeted her as she came into the kitchen. Karen had put her purchases in her bedroom.

"What have you and Molly been doing just now?" Ruth Spanek inquired to her mother.

"We went down to the thrift store is all," Karen answered.

"What do you go down there for anyway?"

"Winter is almost here, and I need something to wear. Besides, I cannot afford to buy new ones."

"Let's fix you some lunch," her mother suggested.

They both sat down to eat sandwiches and make small talk.

"Will you be late getting back from work?"

"The usual closing time, Mom. I am going to study now. I must to keep my grade average up."

"You never get to do anything, Karen," Ruth said, looking at Karen's face.

"Between school and working down at Brown's, I never have time for any social life, Mom." She searched her mother's face for just a hint of sympathy of some sort. Her mother looked as though she wasn't listening to Karen, seeing but not hearing.

Karen went into her room, completing all her homework, saving advertising class for last, her favorite.

She led the class in ad make-up, color, slogans, and an ad campaign. The instructor told her she was a natural in advertising. Time passed quickly. She was to be at Brown's restaurant by six o'clock. She lay down and slept deeply for almost two hours.

She showered and put on her uniform provided by the restaurant. Then she went in to hug her mother at the kitchen table. Ruth was smoking and reading a murder mystery magazine.

"Don't wait up for me, hon. I'm going down to the tavern to play bingo," was all her mother said.

Ten minutes until six, she stepped inside Brown's to a full house of Saturday customers. She looked at the menu board, and then she was ready for work. The evening wore into the night with waves of customers using Brown's for their weekly restaurant choice.

Even though she was very busy, tips were good at twelve dollars and still one hour to go. The waitress shoes were beginning to hurt her feet.

By nine o'clock, Karen had served the last customers—a family of four. The family was enjoying the evening with much bantering among themselves.

How lucky those two children are to have obviously loving parents, she thought.

One day, perhaps this could be for her, Karen dreamed. Karen took off her apron. Mr. Brown paid her, and she walked home.

The house was dark as she let herself inside. She removed her uniform and put on a housecoat. The news was all that was left to watch on television.

Going into her bedroom, she picked an outfit to wear to church the next morning. Minutes later, the outfit selected was pressed, hung up, and ready to be worn. She would get up in time to attend a Baptist church Sunday school of which she was the class president.

Feeling very tired after such a long day, she retired to her bed. Soon, she was fast asleep, not waking when her mother came around twelve thirty. Karen was awakened by her mother in the kitchen, running water, preparing the morning coffee.

She entered the kitchen, asking, "Did you win anything, Mom?"

"Matter of fact, I did, twenty dollars," her mother replied.

"Mom, are you going to church with me this morning?" Karen asked, hoping she wouldn't have to go alone.

"No. I'll fix something for dinner while you're gone," was her mother's answer.

Her mother used to be so alive and loved going to church when Papa was alive. Karen wondered what had caused this big change of habits and personality. Karen ate a bowl of cereal while visiting with her mother.

Tears formed in her mother's eyes. Then she reached for Karen, hugging her. Then she turned away. Trying to explain, Ruth became quiet. In a low voice, she said, "Things are so difficult. I cannot cope with everything."

CHAPTER 2

Karen rose from her chair and took her mother in her arms, saying, "We will always be together. I love you, Mom."

Karen then dressed and left for church. Troubled, she walked the four blocks to church. On the way, she resolved to get a college education, come what may.

Going to her Sunday school, she was greeted by her classmates there. The lesson was on giving. A class project to help a needy family during the holiday was decided upon. Church over, Karen headed home to the smell of a roast as she opened the door.

Her mother greeted her, "Dinner will be ready in a few minutes."

The meal was delicious. The mother and daughter enjoyed it together. Afterward, Karen read the Sunday paper, then studied for two hours.

Monday morning came quickly for Karen. As she got off the city bus in front of Stockton High, her thoughts were on the debating team project Guns in America. She would be the leader of the team, arguing for stricter gun control. The halls were filled with students visiting about their weekend activities.

Mrs. Landers came up to chat and asked Karen if she was prepared for their debate. Karen filled her in on the tack she would take in rebuttal. The holidays were only a few days away.

"One more semester. How will I be able to go on to junior college?" Karen asked herself as she went to her first morning class. The class progressed with note taking and sporadic discussion.

Mrs. Handley went to Karen's desk and handed her a note, saying, "Here is a note from Mrs. Geren. You may skip next class to go see her."

The class finally came to a close. Karen gathered up her books while exchanging small talk with a few of her fellow classmates. She headed to her counselor's office on the second floor.

Karen knocked softly.

"Come in. Hi, Karen, come in, glad to see you got my note," Mrs. Geren said, smiling at her. "Have a seat."

This wonderful, caring person was truly a friend in understanding what Karen's home situation was. Previously in the fall, while in Mrs. Geren's office, Karen began to sob quietly, wondering if it was all right to display this emotion.

At that time, Mrs. Geren came from around her desk to offer her a tissue and hug her.

"You are one of my favorite students in this entire school, and I will help you in any way I can. Furthermore, what is said here stays here behind that door, Karen, I have some fantastic news for you this morning. Our high school has four Grafton Junior College scholarships to offer, and the council of teachers here have picked you as our top recipient," Mrs. Geren said, smiling at Karen with pride and enthusiasm.

"Oh, Mrs. Geren, thank you so much. I want to go on to college so badly but didn't know how I was going to do this. I was only planning to go part-time as I would have to pay my own way," Karen said with tears in her eyes.

"Well, it's books and tuition for the full two years, and it is my pleasure to be the first to tell you. We here at Stockton are so very proud of you," Mrs. Geren finished.

"I'll fill you in on the details in about two months and will announce it in assembly at that time."

"Mrs. Geren, thank everyone, and God bless all of you. I want to go on and get a good college education. This scholarship will help me attain this goal I have set for myself. I work so very hard for my grades."

Karen wiped her eyes and extended her hand toward Mrs. Geren. After Karen left, Mrs. Geren knew the council had made an excellent choice.

Lunch time began for the school, but on the other side of town at the plastic factory, Ruth Spanek left the assembly line for the lunch room.

She and her companion, Iris Campbell, sat down at a table. Both women were brown bagging it after drawing two mugs of coffee from the company urn. They had something in common—single mothers with one teenager at home.

"What did you do this weekend, Ruth?" Iris asked, opening a wrapped bologna sandwich with a bag of chips.

"Went down to Bill's bar. They have bingo down there on Saturday nights," Ruth answered. Ruth looked into her sack. The thirty-minute lunch was typical, too short to relax or rest. The work was hot and fast-paced.

The plastic coming out of the molds was usually several hundred degrees temperature. The average person would be totally wrung out after a day on the line. The work required everyone's constant attention. A bell sounded, and they both began their afternoon shift.

Thank God it's Friday, Ruth thought as the time clock turned four o'clock in the afternoon at Plastic Plus. Assembling plastic containers all day made her hands and back ache. The building was hot from plastic-forming dies.

Huge-wheeled boxes of various plastic assemblies sat row upon row, ready for final work on them. Ruth wore her hair wrapped in a worn blue scarf. She was wearing faded jeans and a short-sleeved knitted matching blouse.

Her shoes were heavy steel-toed work shoes. They were spattered with plastic and dye. Everyone began leaving their work areas, eager to leave the plant.

No one working here could afford anything new, Ruth thought. "Hey, Donna, wait up. I'll walk out with you," Ruth said.

Everyone stood in line to check out. The foreman handed them their weekly checks as they left the building. Donna Meyers, her friend and coworker, walked out with Ruth to her car.

Hesitating, Donna asked, "Ruth, are you going to Bob's to play bingo tonight?"

"Yes, I'm going home to clean up and eat first," Ruth said, starting her car. She felt tired as she drove home.

Ruth parked the car at the garage behind the house. Unlocking the back door, she walked into the kitchen. She looked at the clock on the wall and knew Karen would be at work by now. Then she heated a pot of coffee. She ran her fingers through her stringy shoulder-length hair.

Opening the refrigerator, Ruth took out three containers. She arranged the food on a plate, heating it in a microwave. After eating, she went into the bedroom.

Sitting on the bed, she removed her shoes. Lying down, she quickly fell asleep. An hour later, she awoke, slowly rubbing her eyes.

Undressing, she stepped in the shower. Toweling off, Ruth now stood in front of an open closet deciding what to wear. She began to apply makeup and work on her hair. Who was that woman in her thirties staring back at her? Where had the years gone since Ed died, leaving her with a quiet, intelligent girl?

The sallow face before her had hard-drawn lines. The hair was light brown, having an occasional gray streak in it. Her figure was still thin, thanks to work at Plastic Plus.

Thank heaven Karen had never been any kind of problem. Her daughter studied hard and worked hard. Karen never seemed to be at peace, always driven.

Guess I'll leave her a note before I leave, Ruth thought.

Bathed, dressed, and wearing makeup, she left, locking the backdoor. Maybe she'd get lucky tonight and win some bucks. Two miles later, she parked near other cars around a large bar. A lighted sign said "Bob's." The bar was owned by Bob and Billy Floyd. It was a favorite single blue collar hangout. The jukebox could be heard playing a country and western throbbing heartbreaker. Ruth was looking forward to spending some time with Donna, her closest friend.

She went inside, taking a seat at the bar after being greeted by Bob Floyd. A few regulars began to come in. A group of men were at the bar, laughing and chatting. Their usual banter was about work and wages.

One man in particular gave Ruth the once over. Ray Gould decided before the night was over he would try his luck. This was Friday night, and he just might get lucky.

He sure would like to since his divorce from Nadine four months ago. Nadine just didn't understand him anyway. Ray was employed by Stockton trucking company as a short haul driver.

Ruth sat at the bar, relaxing and trying to unwind from the work week. Later, her friend, Donna, came into Bob's. Donna was a stout-built woman with an outgoing personality. She was raising two children on her own. It seemed she never had a bad day.

Many patrons greeted her as she entered. Everyone knew Donna. She got upon a seat next to Ruth, saying, "Glad to see you here, Ruth." They both sipped draws and made small talk. Ray Gould came over to the bar, introducing himself.

"Ruth, would you care to dance?" he asked.

"Sure, why not?" Ruth replied.

They went out on the crowded dance floor. He was light on his feet, Ruth thought. The song ended, and he walked her back to her seat by Donna, saying, "Thanks, you're a good dancer."

Donna took a sip of her draw and said, "Looks like you've got a good evening going." Everyone bought bingo cards after it was announced.

Donna and Ruth bought two cards each. The cash winning began from $5.00 up to $50.00.

Ruth was missing a win by only one digit. The next game was for $20.00.

Ruth called, "Bingo!"

Everyone called out, "Way to go, Ruth."

The numbers checked out, and Ruth won.

Well, tonight was her lucky night, she grinned, pocketing the Jackson. The game ended an hour later. The jukebox came on again, loud as usual. Both women were having a good time when Ray came over, asking Ruth to dance again. They exchanged job information as they danced.

The night wore on, and both women kept busy dancing it away. Ray asked her if he could give her a call next Friday.

Why not? I'm not getting any younger, Ruth mused. She gave him her home phone number.

By then, Ray had drawn closer as they danced. She smiled up at him. He was six one in his late forties with dark blond hair. His long arms and work-worn hands held her lightly as they went around the floor. Before the last dance, he asked her to go with him on a date the following Saturday.

He was clean-shaven and smelled of aftershave lotion. Ruth agreed to go with him. Ray walked Ruth to her car, said good night, and left. On the way home, she wondered where all this was leading.

Their dancing brought emotions she hadn't felt for a long time. The house was dark and quiet as she looked in on Karen. Ruth slept fitfully that night.

Saturday morning, Ruth rose earlier than Karen. When Karen came into the kitchen, somehow, her mother's demeanor seemed different, more alert.

"Mom, are you all right this morning?"

Ruth appeared to be in another place or time before answering, "Same old me." They both were hungry and ready for breakfast. Ruth quickly made coffee. She then prepared biscuits and gravy for them.

While her mother prepared breakfast, Karen readied the Sunday paper. She began with the comic section.

"How's school and work, honey?" Ruth inquired.

"Next week will be finals, and I'll be glad when they are over," she answered. "My school counselor, Mrs. Geren, told me I've been chosen for a junior college scholarship."

"Karen, I'm so proud of you, working and studying so late at night." Ruth smiled at Karen.

CHAPTER 3

Looking rather sad, Ruth said, "Don't give up on your dreams, Karen."

Karen noticed her mother's eyes moisten up as she talked.

What a rare moment for us, Karen thought. *Why couldn't we always be this close?* Karen wished. *Life isn't about money; it's about loving one another,* Karen so desperately wanted to blurt out.

Together, they cleaned up the kitchen and the house. Ruth did some laundry, then took the car out to have the oil changed. Karen picked out clothing to wear to church. She ironed a blouse, then studied for an hour. She was to work the evening shift at Brown's today.

Karen studied the junior college curriculum, choosing subjects for the first semester. She lay down for a nap and was awakened by her mother's return.

Ruth had bought groceries. She prepared a light lunch for them. Karen was dressed in faded jeans and a dark blue sweatshirt. They sat down to eat.

"What do you have on for tonight, Mom?"

"I think I'll just stay home and keep the twenty I won last night in my pocket," Ruth replied. "Karen, do you need any money?" she asked.

"No, I've been saving for books for this fall."

"You will make your goal because you want to, sweetheart," Ruth said.

This quiet lonely Spartan-like girl, her daughter, just had to make it, Ruth imagined.

Now the time was in December, and the Christmas holidays held everyone's attention. This time of the year was never one of fun and shopping for Karen. This meant more and longer hours at Brown's restaurant.

The free time for her was for laundry, cleaning the house, and studies. Karen was also preparing for the upcoming SAT and ACT tests. She had an excellent memory, which would aid her while taking them.

The good thing about the holidays was that customers' tips were always much better. One evening after arriving home from working at Brown's, Karen noticed her mother was preparing to trim their tree. It was a man-made one.

Though quite tired, she helped her mother finish trimming it. She thought of the presents she would buy, of course one for Molly.

School was finally out for the holidays. Now she could sleep later than usual. Perhaps she and Molly would get to go shopping at one of the local malls. The next morning, she called Molly. They decided to go shopping together the following Monday.

Monday morning, Molly knocked on the front door, ready to go shopping. Karen had finished a considerable amount of housework earlier. She greeted Molly as she shut the door behind her.

"Molly, I must be home in time to go to work this evening," she said, smiling as she got into the car.

"I intend to be gone around two hours," Molly replied, backing out the driveway. A short time later, they parked at an already–filling parking lot. Signs and noises of Christmas were everywhere.

Going inside a large department store, Karen hooked her arm around Molly, asking, "What would you like for Christmas, Molly?"

"Oh, nothing, child. Don't get me anything. You work so hard for your money," she answered her with a smile.

They split up, agreeing to meet later at a designated place. Karen counted her savings for three months. There would be enough for all her purchases.

Now what shall I get Molly and Mother for Christmas, she thought.

The time passed quickly. Her arms were filled with packages. She spotted Molly waiting for her. They went out of the mall chatting excitedly, enjoying each other's company.

Soon they would be home. Arriving home, Karen thanked Molly for the ride and went inside the house. The four presents were for Mr. Highsmith, the bus driver; Mr. Brown at the restaurant, her mother, and Molly. She would later hail Mr. Highsmith and give him his gift.

When he stopped, he asked Karen if she were getting in.

"Not today, Mr. Highsmith. I wanted to give you a Christmas present," she said, handing it to him.

"Why, thank you, Karen, you shouldn't have." He smiled broadly at her.

Well, I don't have any relatives, only good friends like you. Merry Christmas," she said as she stepped off the bus, waving as he drove away.

He was a large man with huge hands, a ruddy face, and blue eyes, always upbeat. Ed's eyes became misty as he drove along while glancing down at the present Karen had given him.

Surely, God would smile on this one today, he thought as he stopped for a fare.

Karen went back inside to get some rest, before going to work later. Her mother had not returned from work as she locked the door before walking to work early in the evening.

Brown's felt cheerful to Karen as she walked in the back door. After removing her coat, she went directly to Mr. Brown and handed him a nicely wrapped present.

"What is this, young lady?" He smiled at her as he continued adding receipts in his office.

"Mr. Brown, I so appreciate everything you have done for me. I don't have a dad anymore, so you will have to do," Karen replied, patting his shoulder.

"Thank you, dear. Anytime I can be of help to you, don't hesitate to ask," he answered. It was a pen and pencil set and a rather expensive organizer. She hoped he would like it.

Business was its normal holiday self, with wall-to-wall hungry customers all evening. Work over, she put on her coat for the chilly walk home. She had asked Mr. Brown if she could take a meal home for her mother. Her mother was at home, still in her work clothes, sitting at the kitchen table, smoking.

Her mother greeted her.

"I brought you home a chicken fry meal. Thought you might be hungry." She sat the covered dish down in front of her mother.

"Thank you, darling. I am sort of hungry," she said, pulling the plate closer to her.

Karen got her some water, a knife, fork, and spoon. She laid her coat on the couch, then sat down at the table visiting with her mother. Then she took off her shoes, rubbing her hurting feet.

"I'm getting a college education so I won't have to do this for the rest of my life," Karen stated.

"How are you going to do that," her mother asked, "between mouthfuls of food?"

"The school gives four junior college scholarships, and I'm going to get one," she answered her mother. "Whatever it takes, I can do because I'll make it somehow. Anyone with high marks in these two tests will be able to get a scholarship."

Karen went into her room to change for bed. Her day had been a long, hard one. Her resolve was to get a quality college education and a better future. She put on a bathrobe and went back into the kitchen to be with her mother.

"What do you want Santa to bring you, Mom?"

"We need so many things, don't get me anything. You work so hard every day," she answered, looking down at her plate. She placed her plate in the sink. "I'm so tired. I'm going to bed. Thanks, sweetheart, for bringing the food home for me." Ruth went in to take a bath before retiring.

One more day, and it would be Christmas. She had purchased a nice dress and a bath set for her mother. She would wrap them tomorrow before leaving for work. Tired as she was, Karen worked on some trigonometry and a Spanish lesson.

A quiet voice broke the night, saying, "Good night, love, don't give up your dreams, Karen." Maybe she could persuade her mother to take some evening computer classes.

The weather had turned cold during the night. The following morning, she heard her mother prepare for work. Karen slept late, which was unusual for her. She got up, going into the kitchen pouring herself a cup of coffee, and then sat down at the table to read the morning paper.

The phone rang. It was her church class. They were to buy groceries for a needy family as a class project.

The group would pick her up around ten o'clock. Karen was ready when they stopped in front of her house. She had written a basic list for family sizes and the amount they had to spend.

One classmate, Larry O'Brien, greeted her, asking, "Karen, where shall we go to buy the grub?"

"Let's go to the Super Saver at Tenth and Corning," she answered. "It's a family of four. They have two children. The father is unable to work," she instructed. "What we will purchase are nonperishable items that can be stored for a length of time." They drove to the grocery store parking lot.

She handed the two boys a list, keeping a list for herself and Sharon Findley. "Please don't buy candy bars, fruit, or anything that will spoil quickly," she stated.

They spread out, using two shopping carts. They would bump into each other as they shopped. An hour passed, and then they checked out, returning three items to the shelf. While checking out, they were eight dollars short, and Karen gave the clerk ten dollars out of her own purse.

They then wheeled the groceries out to Sharon's station wagon. They then drove to the address of the family on their list. They asked Karen to be the one to knock on the door, making the initial approach to the family.

Sharon began to drive toward the north edge of town. Finally, they located the address. A very old car sat in the driveway of a rather run-down house. Two little children peeped through curtains, which needed washing.

Karen said, "Let's say a prayer before we go inside." She led them in a short prayer.

Each of them had groceries in their arms as they walked up to the porch. Karen knocked on the door.

The door opened slowly, and a woman in her early thirties asked, "Can I help you?"

Karen said, "We are members of the senior Bible class from the Baptist church on Third street. We have some food for you today."

The woman saw the four young people loaded with groceries, then began to weep, saying, "Oh, Ted, look."

A soft voice asked, "Who are they, Edna?"

The two children clung to their mother's leg. Sharon spoke to the little children saying, "What's your names?"

"Oh, where are my manners. Do come in," Edna said, wiping her eyes. The group continued unloading the car until all the groceries were inside.

Each spoke to the man in the chair holding a cane, unable to move.

He said, "We thank you so much. God bless you."

They inquired about his injuries. Then Karen asked them if they minded if she said a short prayer. They all joined hands with bowed heads, while Karen led them in a short prayer. The woman thanked them again and hugged each of them.

Sharon drove Karen home first, saying, "See you in church."

Karen waved at them as they drove away. *So many people are worse off than I am,* she thought. Perhaps her class would give this family renewed hope.

Tonight was Christmas Eve. She placed her mother's present under the tree and went off to work. Business wasn't as heavy as it usually had been. Nine o'clock quickly rolled around. Mr. Brown gave her an envelope with her paycheck in it. She would open it later at home.

The house was dark as she entered, turning on the lights. Her mother had not returned home yet. The Christmas tree glowed against the dark of night. She changed into her pajamas and robe, eager to get her uniform and shoes off.

Glancing at the tree, she noticed a rather large package there. Mom had slipped one over on her. At ten thirty, she heard her mother arrive. Karen came out of her room to greet her mother. Her mother was carrying a medium-sizes ham.

"Merry Christmas, Karen. Guess what we will have with our eggs and toast in the morning?" she said, putting the ham in the refrigerator. They both turned in for the night.

The smell of freshly brewed coffee helped Karen wake up. Her mother, dressed in an old faded bathrobe, was sitting at the kitchen table drinking coffee.

"Can we eat before we do anything?" her mother asked.

Her mother quickly had a tasty breakfast of ham, eggs, and toast ready. The breakfast was delicious. It was Friday—Christmas day. She would be home three whole days.

Karen so wished she and her mother could do something together, but nothing came of that idea. Karen gave out the presents. Her mother smiled as never before when she tried on her new dress. She really liked the choice Karen had made.

There was one bulky present still under the tree. It was for Karen. She slowly opened it. It was a very expensive backpack. Her mother looked down at the floor, explaining, "You must have something to carry college books in, you know."

"Never give in or up, dear," was all she added.

She smiled thinly at Karen, giving her a quick hug. The rest of Christmas break passed quickly, and then it was back to the spring semester for Karen.

Mr. Highsmith greeted her upon entering the bus going to school the following Monday. "Thanks for the present, Karen."

Everyone in Stockton High was abuzz with Christmas and New Year's break conversation. Karen's last class for the day was journalism. This was her favorite of all her classes.

Her semester project was a Chevrolet ad for a local dealership. Mr. Colson had also encouraged her to do extra projects—two radio spots and a television spot. He was very pleased with all her work, saying, "You have a genuine flair for advertising, Karen."

CHAPTER 4

Now in February, the days were lengthening. Next week was to be the SAT and ACT tests for seniors of the entire school. The testing room was filled with seniors. The two tests were spread out over two days. The time appeared to just fly by.

Now it was the last of February, and the tests results would be posted on the bulletin board. But Karen's results weren't shown with those posted on the bulletin board. The teacher in her afternoon class handed her a note. She was directed to go see the principal, Mr. Randal. The teacher excused her.

Whatever could be wrong? What had she done wrong? She hesitated before knocking on the principal's outer office door, then entered.

His secretary greeted her, "Let me see if you can go in now." The secretary noticed how tense Karen was and set her at east by saying, "It's going to be something good. You will see. You may go in now, Karen."

Mr. Randal stood up as she entered, greeting her and shaking her hand. Tears came into her eyes while looking at him.

"It's all right, Karen, you have done nothing wrong," he said as he handed her a tissue. "Karen, we here at Stockton are so very proud of you," he began. "In my eighteen years of being principal, this is the most heartening pleasure of my work. Of all the valedictorians we have ever had, you are the most outstanding."

He continued, "You have been selected to be valedictorian of the class of 1998. How do you like that, young lady? I'll make the announcement the second week of next month, plus there will be a typed notice on the main bulletin board. You will also receive a copy of it personally."

He stood again and shook her hand, smiling at her. She brightened up then. He then went over the length and time concerning her valedictorian speech, to be given in May. She arose and left his office, thanking his secretary.

On the way back to her class, she could hardly breathe. She was so excited. The ride home was exciting. She had to tell Mr. Highsmith, cautioning him not to tell until it was official.

He congratulated her profusely, saying, "I'm going to have a VIP riding my bus now."

Karen blushed. She looked at the SAT and ACT scores Mr. Randal had given her. They were 1230 and 32, respectively.

She didn't tell her mother about what had happened that day. Before going to work, she began to outline her speech. It would be based on three basic points. Time passed quickly as she wrote, making changes and corrections.

Then she showered, put on her uniform, and left for work. It was Wednesday, and business was unusually brisk. The evening tips were good, which would be added to her $125.00 savings. Karen knew a considerable amount would be needed for the last years of college. Somehow, she would finish regardless of the sacrifices.

She began walking. Nearing home, a light rain began to fall. A budget began to form in her mind on a monthly and yearly basis. This would help her in setting her goal.

Opening the front door, she saw the lights were on in the kitchen. Ruth was cooking, and it smelled delicious. She had changed into jeans and a pullover sweater.

"Hi, Karen."

"How was work today, Mom?"

"I'm tired, and I have been working on the assembly line all this week."

"Mom, why don't you take an evening class in computers and get out of that place? A computer course will only take ten weeks to finish, and the pay would be around nine dollars per hour."

"I don't know. I'd have to have a lot of new clothes, and I haven't typed since high school," Ruth said, looking away. "Karen, do you want a glass of iced tea? Have you eaten?"

"That sounds great, Mom, all I want to do is just sit for awhile."

Karen and mother visited, sitting at the table, then began cleaning up the kitchen. Karen went to her desk in the bedroom and studied until eleven thirty. She brushed her teeth and went to bed. Her mother had retired much earlier.

April was here now, and it was Friday at Stockman High. Everyone was called to an assembly in the afternoon.

Karen went into the auditorium, sitting with her Communications classmates. Several announcements were made by seniors and the teaching staff, and then a hush came over the auditorium as Principal Randal rose to speak.

"This is the time of the year when our most important announcements of the year are made," he began. "In all the eighteen years I have been principal, we have the most outstanding student ever in Stockman High history as valedictorian," he continued.

"Her scores in SAT and ACT tests were 1230 and 32 respectively," he said, smiling as he looked out over the student body. "This young lady is our own Karen Spank."

The entire assembly broke loose in pandemonium, clapping, yelling, and roaring upon hearing the good news. Her fellow classmates congratulated her.

She was swamped by everyone yelling, "Way to go, Karen." Finally, order was restored. Mr. Sandal had one more announcement.

"Karen will also get a two-year scholarship to attend Grafton Junior College."

She was finally able to get to her locker. All the students swiftly emptied the building, leaving Karen to lug her backpack of books home.

Riding home, she told Mr. Highsmith, "It's official now, Mr. Highsmith, I'm valedictorian."

She wished her mother were home to hear the good news. But Ruth didn't return until Karen was off work after nine thirty that night. Karen was waiting for her as she heard her mother park her car in the garage.

Ruth entered and shut the back door. She looked at Karen, wondering what she was doing sitting at the kitchen table so quiet. Karen placed the typed announcement on the table in front of her mother.

"What's this all about, Karen?" Ruth read the announcement through. "Oh, honey, look at what you've done!" She smiled and whooped. "Stand up and let your mother hug a big winner."

Karen grinned from ear to ear. "Mother, would you do me a big favor?"

"Anything, honey, right now." Ruth continued to smile as she hugged Karen.

"Please go to the graduation to see me give my valedictorian speech," Karen asked, weeping.

"Honey, you know I will, and I promise to be there with bells on. We will have to buy a graduation dress, Karen."

"Molly has already finished sewing it two days ago," she said, looking at Ruth. "Molly said that it would be her gift to me for graduation. She is a good seamstress, Mother," Karen finished.

"Well, I'm so proud of you, Karen Sue Spanek," Ruth said, smiling at her, and hugged her again. "You've worked so hard night after night, studying late every night. You've earned it, dear," her mother said. They both retired for the night.

Warm weather brought May in Stockton with blooming flowers. The big buzz around Stockton High was the Friday night prom.

Larry O'Brien came up to Karen in front of her locker. He was shy and hesitant. "Hi, Karen, how are you doing?" he asked. She noted he had something important on his mind. "Karen, would you go to the prom with me Friday night?" he blurted out.

Her face reddened slightly at the question. She had never dated before and felt out of place.

"Oh, Larry, I've never dated, and I work all the time. I'm afraid I wouldn't be very much fun," she said apologetically.

"That's all right, Karen, I don't date either. I'd just like to go and see everyone." He looked inquiringly at her. "I can get my dad's car, and I'll treat you nice as we go to church together. Look, we won't stay out late. We will come straight home afterward."

"On one condition, that it will be my treat for something to eat afterward."

"Okay, I'll pick you up at seven, Friday evening."

"See you Friday then, Larry," she said as she closed her locker door.

Dating wasn't in her future, but she had known Larry O'Brien for years. Perhaps this one time would be okay. She would go over to Molly's house to get her new dress to wear on Friday.

She finally arrived home going over to Molly's, knocking on the door.

Molly came to the door, smiling at her and saying, "Come in, dear."

"Guess what, Molly, I'm valedictorian of the class of 1998 at school. That's not all, I've got a date for the Friday night prom," she stated breathlessly.

"Honey, your dress is ready. Why don't you try it on?" Molly asked. "You can change in the bedroom. It will only take a few minutes," she said, pointing at the bedroom.

"Do you think I could wear it to the prom, Molly?"

"You could, but I have just the thing for you to wear, sweetie."

Karen returned, wearing the new dress. It fit perfectly and looked beautiful. "What do you mean, Molly?"

Molly went into a large closet, returning with a dress wrapped in a plastic cover.

"Here, help me take this out of this plastic," she said, pulling the cover off.

There, was a gorgeous yellow formal Molly was holding up for Karen to see.

"It will fit you, Karen, and it hasn't been worn but once. I have a pair of matching shoes."

Karen went back into the bedroom to try the formal on. She came back into the room modeling the beautiful gown, which fit nicely. Molly smiled broadly at her young friend.

"Wear this gown, and you won't turn into a pumpkin, dear," Molly chided. The gown was new and looked wonderful on Karen, contrasting with her dark auburn hair. Karen whirled around the room, delighted with it. The shoes fit nicely also.

Karen went to Molly and hugged her, saying, "How can I ever thank you, Molly? Please come to my graduation." She thanked Molly again and left to go home.

She would somehow fix her hair for the coming prom with Larry. The rest of the week went quickly after asking Mr. Brown for Friday evening off.

Arriving home, Karen dumped her backpack on her desk. She began to plan the rest of the day. She ate something before showering and getting ready for the evening.

Larry knocked on her door promptly at seven o'clock as promised. Karen answered his knock, saying, "Come in for a minute. I'll have to leave my mother a note." Larry was dressed in a suit and tie, looking very nice. She left a note, placing it on the kitchen table.

Her mother still had not gotten home from work. *Chances are, I'll get home before my mother anyway,* Karen thought.

"Gee, you look beautiful in that gown, Karen," Larry remarked. "Here is a corsage I brought for you." He handed it to her. She had him help pin it on her gown. They did indeed look quite the handsome young couple. He held the door for her, and they went outside.

The prom was being held at the school gymnasium. When they arrived, it was filled with wall-to-wall students. A popular local band was playing. Karen and Larry were greeted by everyone, surprised to see Karen so beautifully dressed. Karen was greeted by many teachers and students.

They both had fun, dancing and visiting with other groups attending. Finally, everyone crowded the dance floor for the last dance of the evening.

Leaving the prom, Karen took Larry's arm as they walked to his car.

"Thanks for asking me, Larry, I've had such a good time," Karen said, getting into the car.

"You deserved to go tonight. You work so very hard, Karen," Larry added.

"Now, Larry, take us to a nice place to eat, my treat."

They drove to Duffs, the most popular place for young people to hang out in Stockton. They went inside with Larry holding the door for Karen. They found a booth and sat down. A waitress came by to take their order, which were burgers, fries, and drinks. They soon got caught up in what they would be doing in the future.

Larry talked about a degree in engineering, while Karen explained about radio and television work. They got up to leave, with Karen picking up the check. She paid, and they left for Karen's house.

The lights were on inside. Larry went in to meet her mother and found Ruth sitting at the kitchen table.

"Aren't you two quite the handsome couple? Did you two have a good time?"

"We danced every dance and had the best time ever," Larry answered as Karen introduced him to her mother.

"I really must go home, Karen," Larry said.

"I'll walk you out, Larry."

Outside, Larry stood close to Karen touching her side, then drew her to him in a quick embrace. Then he said, "Good night, Karen, you are a very sweet person."

After he left, Karen went back inside to visit with her mother.

"My, but you look so elegant in that gown, honey." Ruth looked at Karen with an approving look.

How busy the last week of school has been, Karen thought, *particularly the last three days.* Her classes were finished, and she would be graduating this coming Friday at the Stockton High School stadium. She had spent many hours polishing her valedictorian speech.

CHAPTER 5

Molly and Ruth were going together to the graduation ceremonies. Each day, Karen returned home with more items in her backpack accumulated in her four years at school.

Mr. Brown had already informed her she could work full-time during the summer. She would save as much money as she could at this time.

Wednesday, she went into Mrs. Geren's office to be briefed on the details of her scholarship at Grafton Junior College.

Mrs. Geren smiled at her as she entered the office, greeting Karen, "Hi, Karen, I'm looking forward to your speech Friday evening. Sit down and let's go over your scholarship together." Mrs. Geren went over books, tuition, type of courses, and where the school was located.

"Will college courses be difficult, Mrs. Geren?" Karen asked.

"Karen, you will ace all your courses because you prepare so well," Mrs. Geren assured her. "Going to a junior college will help you go on to any four-year college in this state or anywhere else."

"Thank you for all these four years that you have been here for me," Karen said, standing to leave.

"Come by anytime I can help," Mrs. Geren replied.

Karen would miss this wonderful, caring woman. *Perhaps I can share a ride with someone also going to Grafton,* she thought as she walked from the building.

There was no reason for her to return to school in the morning. She would go to Grafton Junior College to get a bulletin of all the courses and schedules they offered next week. While there, she would inquire about the freshman classes required.

Karen had already decided on a major in communications and a minor in journalism. An estimate formed in her mind about her junior and senior year costs. Arriving home, Karen went next door to return Molly's gown and shoes. Molly greeted her at the door.

"See, you didn't turn into a pumpkin after all. Come on in," she said, holding the door open for her.

"Thank you so much, Molly. You will always be in my heart and mind."

"You are like the daughter I never had," Molly replied. They sat and visited for a time. Karen told Molly about her scholarship to Grafton Junior College.

"You certainly are bound and determined," Molly said.

"Now you are coming to my graduation, aren't you?"

"Wouldn't miss it for anything, dear," Molly assured her.

"Well, I must go home as I have to go to work tonight," Karen said, trying to leave.

She went home to lie down and rest before going to work later in the evening. Her cap and gown were on a hanger in her bedroom.

Friday afternoon was a busy time for Karen. She pressed out any wrinkles left in her new dress. Then she rehearsed her speech that she would give that evening. Ruth arrived home from work and hurriedly prepared a meal for herself and Karen.

The phone rang at that moment, and Ruth answered it. "We will be ready to leave at ten minutes to seven. Okay? That was Molly wanting to know when we will leave," she filled Karen in on the details. "I know you must be there early, Karen. I have to check the film in my camera."

Ruth went to get ready. She bathed and put on her best dress. She looked better than Karen had seen her in a long time. She was proud of her mother at that moment. After dabbing some perfume on, Ruth picked up her purse. Ruth and Karen were both ready and waiting. The time was 6:30 p.m.

Karen looked so beautiful in her cap and gown, Ruth thought, admiring her. She took a shot of Karen. She was so proud of her. There was a knock at the door, breaking her reverie. It was Molly. She was holding a camera.

"Now Karen, let's get some shots of you in your cap and gown." She clicked the shutter as she lined up each shot.

They got into Ruth's car and left for the stadium, a few minutes away. They were all quiet as they drove to the stadium. The sun was at a lower angle as it gleamed on the stadium. They parked, and then Karen left Molly and her mother to line up with her classmates.

The entire staff was assembled on the platform, wearing their caps and gowns. Mrs. Geren came down the line and asked Karen to follow her to the platform. Karen was asked to join the staff on the platform. One of the staff rose and went to the podium to present the graduating class of 1998.

Following this, a prayer was given by a local minister. Karen was seated to the right of the dignitaries. Her mother rose from her seat to go forward, taking several shots of Karen. Karen smiled as she hadn't seen her mother that interested in years.

Several announcements were made by the staff. Next, Principal Randal made a few remarks, the last was presenting Karen, "Karen S. Spanek is our valedictorian for the class of 1998 with SAT and ACT scores of 1233 and 32, respectively while maintaining a *3.75* grade average during her four years of high school.

"These scores are the highest we have had in fifteen years," he continued. "It is with great pleasure I present Ms. Karen Spanek." He then turned, smiled, and began to clap. The entire audience responded. Then he shook her hand as she approached the podium.

Ruth, having heard all these accolades about her own daughter, began to feel tears springing from her eyes. *Why couldn't I have been a better mother to this beautiful, intelligent person?*

Karen went to the podium, and placing the folder containing her speech on it, said, "Thank you, Principal Randal, the teaching staff at Stockton, my fellow classmates, parents, and families gathered here this evening. To say the least, this makes me feel most humble.

"There are two topics I would like to cover this evening in my remarks. They are appreciation and future. Lexicographers tell us appreciation means grateful recognition. Future noun form—the time that is to come.

"We students should appreciate what sacrifices our parents have made for us. Try to walk a mile in their shoes. When was the last time you told your parents you loved them? Scare them to death by saying, 'I'm sorry to have been such a pain in the neck.' Clean your room. They will probably take your temperature. Look at them this moment. How so very lucky you are. What would America be without that glue called parents and family? Our teachers are next on the appreciation list.

"All who have taught you have spent a lifetime preparing to teach. Almost all of them have two or three degrees. What would possess them to spend hours in a stuffy classroom teaching? They do this because it's a very special calling, trying to interest you in preparing for a future. They know our knowledge is ever expanding. Our true Olympics are with the many countries ahead of us in almost every category of learning.

"These teachers are preparing you for tomorrow. Have you been taking baby steps or giant steps toward this time? The future or rather our tomorrow can never be realized if we don't act swiftly and strongly. Your alumni meetings future-wise will only be gauged by how you face the future challenges. Where will you be ten years from now? Will you sleep as Rip Van Winkle did?

"Why would you not care about your position in the race called the future? You are the ruler of your tomorrow. We know you only receive by what you have given. I was unable to sleep the last few nights. A short poem kept me awake, thinking of these few lines: 'Why wait to speak of cheer to those you hold dear. If you must have to part, speak softly from the heart. Before you travel very far, ere a loved one has passed the bar.' To my fellow classmates, may God show you the path and light your way into the future. May God bless you. Thank you." Karen finished then returned to her seat.

The entire audience stood up, cheering and clapping for her. The graduation exercises continued by calling the graduating class's names alphabetically. Finally, the last one crossed the stage. The faculty congratulated Karen on her speech.

Her mother came near the platform and took several more shots of Karen. Going down into the audience, she was greeted by everyone.

"You did well with your speech, honey," her mother said.

Molly also came up to take pictures of Karen. Karen was mobbed by many of her classmates wishing her well. They had her sign their annuals.

"You've got high school over with anyway."

"In a way, it's only the beginning because I've four years of college to finish."

They got in Ruth's car and drove home, whereupon Molly thanked them for the ride.

"Thanks again, Molly, for the pretty dress, I appreciate it," Karen said.

Karen and her mother went inside. The time was ten o'clock. They changed into their nightgowns, then went into the kitchen for a snack.

After visiting and snacking, they both turned in for the night. The next morning, Ruth prepared a true breakfast feast. They enjoyed one mother's company. They worked together cleaning up the house. Early afternoon, Karen changed into her uniform.

She then walked to Brown's restaurant. Mr. Brown made a special effort to congratulate Karen about being class valedictorian

"We really have a celebrity working here," he said proudly.

Going into the main dining room, she saw a sign displayed there. It read, "Congratulations to our own Karen S. Spanek, Valedictorian of the Class of 1998 of Stanton High."

Karen fell silent as she read it. Then everyone there clapped for her diners and workers alike. She was slightly embarrassed.

The evening was very busy with a continual swell of customers until closing. She asked Mr. Brown if she could have the sign after it was taken down. It was a beautiful evening as she walked home. She felt lost without a huge load of studies.

Her mother was gone, and she was home alone. She read the paper and watched television late, then turned in for the night. Around midnight, she heard her mother come in quietly.

The next morning—Sunday—Karen read the classified ads. One ad in particular caught her eye. "Share ride to Grafton Junior College summer session, late model car." Karen dressed for church, leaving around 9:15 for her Sunday school class. Several of her classmates said, "Hi, Karen, way to go on being valedictorian."

After Sunday school was over, she sat with Sharon Finley's family, where Mrs. Finley greeted her. This was an ordinary blue-collar family, dressed in their Sunday best. Karen felt at ease with them.

The pastor led the congregation in an opening prayer. A deacon of the church made some church announcements. The pastor then took the lectern.

"Before beginning my morning message, I have a few words about one of our own high school graduates," he said smiling. "Would you please put your hands together for our own Karen Spanek, 1998 school valedictorian," he added. The entire congregation clapped loudly for her.

"God is surely working among our members this day," he continued. His message was about serving our fellow man.

Church over, Karen declined a ride home offered her by the Finley's. She walked home slowly, thinking of her future. Surely, a good education would be the key to her future.

Arriving back home, Karen could smell food being cooked. Ruth had prepared a fine dinner. Karen changed her clothes, ready for the rest of the day. They sat down to eat, making small talk during the meal. She helped her mother clear the dishes.

Later, she sat on the sofa, reading the classified ads in the Stanton Gazette. She reread the ad concerning a rider going to Grafton Junior College. She went to the telephone and dialed the number in the ad.

A brassy voice answered, "Prathers."

"I am calling about your ad in the Gazette," Karen stated.

"That's my ad. I'm Tiffany Prather," the voice answered.

"Are you taking summer courses at Grafton?"

"Yes, I am. Are you going this summer too?"

"Yes, if I could get a ride to and from the campus. I would like to take Western Civilization."

"Let's get together today," Tiffany suggested. "What's your address? I'll be right over."

Karen gave Tiffany her address. Thirty minutes later, a young woman drove up in a red Chevrolet Alumna. Karen opened the door and went outside. The driver was strawberry blond, tall, and with a positive smile as she got out of the car. She had light skin peppered with occasional freckles. Her green eyes were her outstanding feature setting off her face. Tiffany exuded positive attitude and was easy to like. The two girls were friends right away, bonding quickly. One girl with dark hair, blue eyes, and classic features; the other with brassy blond hair, pretty features. The blond was all legs and big frame. Her personality was very pleasant and outgoing.

CHAPTER 6

"Hi, Karen, I'm Tiffany Prather", she said, holding out her hand.

"Come inside, let's visit," Karen said, smiling up at her. They went into the front room where Karen introduced Tiffany to her mother.

"Mind if I smoke?" Tiffany asked as she lit up a cigarette.

"What is your major going to be, Tiffany?"

"I want to be a counselor."

The two girls chattered like magpies for well over an hour, obviously enjoying the time together. Both decided on the first week of June to enroll in courses at Grafton. They finally concluded their conversation. Tiffany said good-bye to Ruth before going outside. Tiffany offered Karen a reasonable fee for riding with her.

Tiffany said, "I hate to attend by myself. I will call you before Monday, June the first. See you later," she said as she got in her car and drove away. Karen waved at her new friend.

Karen couldn't *wait* for June to arrive. Meanwhile, she worked every day at Brown's, saving as much money as possible for books and fees that would be needed. She had saved enough money for the summer session at Grafton. One Sunday afternoon, the phone rang. It was Tiffany calling.

"I'll pick you up around nine o'clock, Monday morning, Karen."

"I'll be ready and waiting." They chatted for more than thirty minutes.

Monday morning, Karen rose early and got ready for the day. She had been reading through a Grafton college course bulletin. She was prepared when Tiffany arrived on time, with the car radio playing rock and roll.

Tiffany grinned at Karen, saying, "Get in, let's go. I couldn't wait to see you again. This will be fun."

"I must be home by four o'clock this afternoon. I work at Brown's restaurant. I've worked there for three years."

"That's hard work."

Karen began to tell about the loss of her father. Then finished relating how difficult everything had been for her mother. She felt a sense of relief after telling Tiffany about her life. She ended, saying, "I want to get a good college education. My major will be in communications and a minor in journalism."

"You and I are alike, as I want a good education also. Whatever it takes and no matter how long it takes, I'm getting an education."

Tiffany told Karen about her parents. "All they do is work. They never go anywhere. I earned this car by working in Lowes station. I'm getting an education so living will be easier. So it's on to college for me."

The rest of the trip was spent getting better acquainted. Neither had time nor wanted to date. This would be the beginning of a lifetime friendship for them.

After a twenty-five-minute drive, they arrived at the junior college. On the rock wall at entrance, a metal plate read "Grafton College." It had an excellent reputation, having been founded by Russell B. Grafton, a multimillionaire long since dead.

They drove past many campus buildings. Some were dormitories. On the edge of the campus was a large sports stadium. Tiffany parked in front of the registration building.

Karen had brought along all the records necessary for attending summer classes. She went to a different area than Tiffany to register. She was waited upon by an older woman with graying hair. The woman took extra time reading through Karen's high school records.

"I'm Edna Philstrom. I register freshmen and will help in any way I can. Karen, my dear, you have been one busy girl. I am impressed by your background." She smiled at Karen, continuing, "Congratulations, Karen, these are the best records I've seen in many years. I notice you have a full scholarship here at Grafton. You're going to get Western Civilization out of the way this summer session. An excellent idea," Mrs. Phil Philstrom commented.

After several cards were typed out and fees collected, Karen was enrolled in Grafton for summer classes.

"Karen, you won't have any problems here at Grafton," Mrs. Philstrom stated.

"I have worked so hard to make those grades. I want a good college education Mrs. Philstrom," Karen replied.

Edna Philstrom could see a determination in this quiet, plainly dressed girl. There seemed to be a lonely sadness about her. "Anytime I can help, please call on me, Karen," she said.

Soon, Karen was joined by Tiffany. They had classes during the same hours. They went to buy some used texts at the campus bookstore. The bookstore was in a nearby building.

Karen purchased a used Western Civilization book in good condition. Tiffany also found a book she needed for her class. Karen was anxious to get home as it was already three thirty. They drove home talking about their summer classes.

Arriving at Karen's house, Tiffany said, "I'll pick you up around nine thirty on Monday morning."

Karen asked, "May I pay you each week for my ride?"

"How about a dollar each day?"

"That's great, see you Monday then."

"It will be a great summer, Karen," Tiffany said, before driving away.

Karen went inside and fixed a glass of iced water to drink. Sitting on the sofa, she leafed through the text she had purchased.

Quickly, she drifted off to sleep. Later, she awoke with a start. She began to get ready to go to work at Brown's that evening. While walking to Brown's, she thought, *just once, I'd like to do what I please—not work.*

Monday morning, Karen was waiting out front for Tiffany. Minutes later, Tiffany drove up, smiling at Karen as she got in the car.

"Did you do anything special this weekend?" Tiffany inquired.

"No, I only looked through the text and went to church," Karen explained.

"I should go to church, but I never seem to get up early enough," Tiffany said as she drove across town.

"Go with me to my church next Sunday. I go to a nearby Baptist church."

"Okay."

The two girls visited as they rode along, enjoying each other's company. They drove up the winding lane to the college. Tiffany parked in the Grafton student parking lot. Both girls got out, going their separate ways.

"See you at the car after classes."

"Okay," Tiffany returned.

Karen's class was rather small. Everyone dressed very casual. The instructor was a woman in her late forties. Her name was Mrs. Esther Bolinger. She began by calling the class roll.

Then she outlined what the course was and what was expected of each student. Karen was the youngest class member. There were only fifteen students in the class.

The class was an accelerated one due to the short summer session. Mrs. Bolinger began to go into the course immediately. There would be many pages to cover before next Friday. At ten o'clock, Karen's class was finished for the day.

Karen gathered up her notes and book, then went to the campus parking lot. It was a beautiful June day. Karen could see Tiffany walking toward the car.

"How was your first class?" Karen asked.

Tiffany gave a rundown on the psychology class she was taking. "Let's go swimming some afternoon," Tiffany suggested. The two new friends continued riding to class and learning more about each other.

Karen was maintaining a straight four-point grade average in her classes. Tiffany was also doing nicely in her classes.

In July, they each brought something to eat for a picnic they had planned. On another day after class, they went swimming. They lay in the sun, talking about their future plans, sharing confidences.

Gradually, the summer wore on, and the classes came to an end during the month of August. Before leaving for the summer, they went in to enroll for their fall classes. Karen asked to talk with Mrs. Philstrom.

"Come into my office, Karen, I will get you enrolled for the fall semester," Mrs. Philstrom said.

She had Karen's folder in front of her. She took a few minutes to review Karen's background. Then she looked up at Karen and smiled.

"The Western Civilization class didn't hold you up at all. You made an A in it I see."

Mrs. Philstrom explained the scholarship program Karen was attending with. She helped Karen enroll in the courses that were required.

Karen's summer classes were finished. The two and a half months seemed to fly by. She had become accustomed to studying each day after class. The classes were much faster and accelerated.

Tiffany and Karen became closer as friends. They were indeed opposites in personality. Karen was quiet, whereas Tiffany was forward and outspoken.

They found time from work to share a picnic together. Often, they would go swimming and talk about their goals. Both girls enjoyed the moments they shared.

Karen's schedule usually meant she would have to be home by late afternoon. Tiffany continued her work at a local Quik-Trip store.

In one week, the fall classes were to begin. The two friends drove to Grafton one morning to purchase the books they would need. Karen was given a voucher for her books as part of her scholarship program. Tiffany noticed the voucher in Karen's hand.

"What's that for, Karen?"

"It pays for my books through my scholarship."

"You mean you got a full ride the entire two years here at Grafton?"

"Yes, but I'll lose it if I don't keep my grades up."

"Who was your class valedictorian, Karen?"

"I was Stanton High's valedictorian and also received one of the three scholarships."

Tiffany was in awe of Karen and hugged her. "You deserve it, Karen, you work so hard studying. Now I understand why you're so driven."

"Tiffany, I study hard because I want to make something of myself. An education is what I'm after."

"I want to help people untangle their lives. That's why I'm taking the courses for counseling. My next degree will be a masters."

Finally, Tiffany stopped at Karen's house. Karen struggled with a load of books.

"Karen, I'll pick you up for the first classes next month. Bye now. Call me, Karen, I'll be home in the mornings."

The next three weeks dragged by with only occasional phone calls between them. Karen scanned her college texts. She saved all she dared from her salary and tips.

Karen got up early one morning to go through her clothes. She threw out any that didn't fit or was too worn. She went next door to visit Molly.

Molly came to the door and smiled to see Karen standing there. "Hi, sweetheart. Have you been busy going to college?"

"Molly, I took Western Civilization to get it behind me. I'm taking courses every summer to get out quicker. Molly, let's go to the thrift store soon."

"Come in and let's visit. How about a glass of tea first?"

They went into Molly's kitchen. Molly prepared iced tea for them. Soon, they were chatting away. They decided to go to the thrift store Thursday morning.

On Thursday morning, Karen finished her housework and went over to Molly's house. Molly stepped outside and locked her front door. They got into Molly's car to leave. Riding in Molly's car, they soon parked in front of the thrift store. They shopped together. Molly showed Karen several pieces that were like new.

The pieces of clothing Karen selected would get her through the school year. They stopped to have burgers and fries. Molly asked Karen more about her summer classes. They finished, then drove to Molly's.

Karen looked at Molly and smiled at her, saying, "Thanks, Molly, I love you dearly."

"It's my pleasure, Karen. Call on me anytime."

Molly well understood how difficult life was for Karen. She had a mother who showed little concern for her. Any other mother would be delighted to have Karen as a daughter. *Why?* Molly thought. *This child went to church and did all the right things. Why?*

Karen carried her purchases into the house. She matched different articles together, thus creating a wider wardrobe.

On morning, late in August, Karen heard a knock, and she saw Tiffany standing there. She asked Tiffany in. They both visited for a few minutes.

"Tiffany, let's go next door. I want you to meet my friend Molly."

They went next door and knocked on Molly's door. Molly answered the door and was surprised and delighted to see them. She invited them in. Karen introduced Tiffany to Molly. Molly could see the friendship between the two girls. They complimented one another nicely.

Karen was quiet, whereas Tiffany was forward. She enjoyed talking with them. Tiffany was good for Karen, she thought.

CHAPTER 7

The girls got up to leave, said good-bye, and left. Fall and football arrived in Stanton. Classes began for Karen. They would require more time and preparation. She only wished her work at Brown's wouldn't take up so many evening hours.

The days and weeks went by so quickly for Karen. It appeared to be like a blur. Christmas was a short time away. Karen would purchase presents for the people in her life. Christmas holidays were like most other ones, except no classes.

Semester ending, papers were due soon. During the holidays, Tiffany and Karen attended a movie together. They had already enrolled in their spring classes. They both had maintained high grades in all their classes.

The spring semester was about to end for them. In one month, they would have finished a year at Grafton. Nature was breaking out everywhere. Trees were leafing out and flowers blooming.

They discussed renting an apartment for their junior and senior years at Capitol City University. Tiffany and Karen spent more time together. They went swimming when their work permitted. The spring semester passed by so quickly for Karen. She would take another summer class and continue working at Brown's. Her standing was a second semester sophomore, and her grades were a 4.0.

Between working at Brown's and college studies, Karen didn't see much of her mother. One evening after work, Ruth was sitting in the living room, just watching television.

Greeting Karen, she said, "How did it go this evening, kiddo?" It seemed her mother needed to confide in her, or perhaps just talk. How long had it been since they had any conversation or exchange of words?

"We had a huge crowd, and I earned eighteen dollars in tips," Karen answered as she sat down in an easy chair.

Ruth hesitated, searching for the right words to say to Karen. "Recently, I got acquainted with a guy at Bill's bar," she began. "We have been dating some. His name is Ray Gould."

"Mom, you need to get out and date," Karen said, looking at her mother in a positive way. She took off her shoes and relaxed, not moving. A few minutes later, Karen went into her bedroom and got ready for bed.

The summer went along with the same routine as many years before for Karen and Tiffany. They did as many things as could together, work permitting.

Karen was still riding with Tiffany to her summer classes. She was well ahead of her required college hours to graduate at Grafton. The two girls' friendship grew during these past two years and would last a lifetime for them.

One evening after returning home, Karen stayed up late working on a class paper. It was past midnight. Her mother had never stayed out that late before.

Ruth came home early the next morning. She was sitting at the kitchen table quietly sipping coffee, not explaining where she had been. Karen came into the kitchen in a housecoat. Her mother got up to pour her a cup of coffee.

Ruth spoke abruptly, "Karen, Ray asked me to marry him, and I said yes. We could use a man around the house for a change." She waited for Karen to reply.

"When are you getting married, Mom?"

"Next Friday up at City Hall."

"This seems rather sudden, but you've known him for about a year."

"Karen, we will be a real family again, honey."

Karen had misgivings since she had never met Raymond Gould. Would this marriage change the relationship between mother and daughter?

The following weekend, Karen got to meet him. It was Saturday morning when she answered a knock at the door. She opened the door, and there stood a large built man. He had dirty blond hair and a ruddy complexion and looked like a tough. He wore cowboy boots and worn jeans.

He had a leering, stupid grin as he looked her over. Was this her mother's prince charming?

"Hi, you must be Karen. Is your mother home?" He kept grinning as he introduced himself. He tried to draw her to him, trying to hug her. She stepped away from him. Just then, Ruth came to the front of the house, smiling at Ray. She hugged him, keeping her arm about his waist.

"Here's my man, Karen," Ruth said.

They walked into the kitchen and sat down at the table. "Ruth, you didn't tell me your daughter was this cute," Ray exclaimed. He was trying to ingratiate himself with Karen.

They drank coffee and visited, with Ray asking Karen about school. He kept eyeing Karen. His mannerisms put her on guard. When Karen rose to leave, he tried to put his arm around her waist.

All during this time, Ruth wasn't noticing his real purpose. Karen heard them talking about his moving into their home. The following Friday was to be their wedding day, but neither of them included Karen in the ceremony. Her mother was thinking only of herself.

The week went by quickly for Karen. After work, Karen walked home dejected. Her mother was getting married in the morning.

She let herself in with her key. The house was quiet and dark. She changed into her pajamas and studied quite late. She hadn't heard from her mother for two days.

Friday afternoon, Karen arrived home from school. She had just sat down when Ray and her mother came into the house. They were both dressed in their best clothes. Ruth had a corsage pinned to her lapel. Ray and Ruth were holding each other and kissing.

"Hi, Karen. Aren't you going to congratulate us?" her mother asked.

"Don't be such a spoil sport, kid," Ray said.

"Neither of you asked me to be any part of it," Karen replied. "Who do you think I am, mashed potatoes?" Karen asked grimly.

"Now, honey, I didn't think you could get away from school," Ruth returned.

Ray tried to pull Karen up from the couch, but she moved out of his reach.

"You're not going to refuse your new daddy a kiss, are you?" Ray asked. She could smell liquor on their breaths.

"Sweetie, my new husband and I are going to Bill's bar and celebrate. Aren't we, Ray? Do you want to come with us tonight?"

"No, I have to go to work at five," Karen said, holding back tears. Ruth and Ray left for Bill's bar. Karen went next door to Molly's house.

Molly heard a knock at the door and opened it. There stood Karen trying not to cry. "Come in, come in, and talk to me, child," Molly told her. She flew into Molly's arms. Molly kissed her on the cheek while hugging her. "What's the matter, sweetheart?"

"My mother got married today and didn't even ask me to be there."

"Let's go into the kitchen and have a glass of iced tea."

Karen could see that Molly had been sewing on something. Molly poured tea for them.

"Close your eyes now darling. I've got something to show you!" Karen quickly closed her eyes, not cheating.

"You may open your eyes now," Molly instructed.

There in Molly's hands was the most beautiful dress Karen had ever seen. It was to be her junior college graduation dress that Molly had previously talked about.

"Oh, Molly, it's so pretty. I love it!" Karen gasped.

"Dry those tears, love, and try it on right now."

Karen went into a back bedroom and changed into the new dress.

It fit like a glove, every stitch and button in place. *No store had a dress as fine as this one*, she thought.

Molly was pleased with the fit of the dress. Karen did a turn, modeling it for Molly. Karen removed the dress, placing it on a hanger. She went to Molly, saying, "Thank you, you are my very best friend."

Molly listened to Karen relate the happenings at her house. Molly knew of Ray Gould's reputation, and that he had been married three times before.

She didn't want to say anything to Karen about her thoughts. This young girl was in for some problems, Molly surmised.

Karen arose, saying, "Thanks again for my graduation dress, Molly. I love you." She was due at Brown's soon, so she told Molly good-bye and left.

Things had eased somewhat at home. Ruth had become more cheery after the marriage. Meals were more regular now. Ray was good with his hands, repairing everything in sight. He had almost finished painting the outside of the house.

He still would make a play for Karen when Ruth wasn't near. Karen avoided these times as best she could.

Tiffany and Karen talked about home life while driving to school. They shared their problems. Karen explained about Ray and his behavior with her.

Both girls had signed up for summer classes again. Karen was taking advertising and television courses and doing well in them. She was on the Dean's honor roll. Advertising was her most promising subject.

Her instructor, Don Lorton, asked Karen to see him after school. She went into his office and sat down. "Karen, the reason I called you in is about a part-time job," he said, smiling at her. "Your grades and enthusiasm makes you a perfect candidate for this job. It's an advertising job with KSOK here in the city. You will be developing advertising similar to what you are doing here in class. Would you be able to go out to the station today for an interview?"

"I sure can, and thank you so much for recommending me," Karen said, thanking him and shaking his hand.

She read the memorandum in her hand. Waiting in the car, she could hardly wait to tell Tiffany. Tiffany's class was just finished now, and she was approaching the car.

"Tiffany, I have a job offer from the television station KSOK."

"No kidding. That's on my way, Karen, let's go. You deserve a break, go for it." They stopped at Karen's while she quickly changed clothes. A short time later, they arrived at the KSOK station.

"Do you want me to wait for you, Karen?" Tiffany asked.

"No, that won't be necessary." She thanked Tiffany and went inside. A secretary took her name and then disappeared down a hall.

She came back shortly and told Karen to follow her. She was escorted into the station manager's office. A rather short, balding man in his forties held out his hand, saying, "I'm Myron Decker." Karen shook his hand. He asked her to take a seat.

He looked over her brief resume. He sat for a few minutes, deep in thought. Then he looked up and smiled at Karen.

"Wow, young lady, you are some kind of powerhouse!" He asked her about high school and college projects. "I've talked with all of your school instructors, and I want you to work for us here at KSOK. We could like you to begin Monday after your college classes. Do you have any questions before you leave?"

"I only want to say I'll work hard and uphold your confidence in me."

Mr. Decker began to go over the hours and her wages of $9.00 an hour, also discussing station policy. Karen arose and shook his hand once more, thanking him for the opportunity.

"You'll do fine I'm sure, Karen. See you Monday afternoon."

Only one thing was on her mind as she went home on the bus. She must tell Mr. Brown, who had been like family to her. She got off the bus near her house with a heavy heart. How would she tell him about the big change in her working life? Arriving home, she showered and put on a clean uniform, then left for her evening work.

The evening crowd was large, and it was a busy evening for everyone. When the evening was over, Karen went into Mr. Brown's office. He was in his office working.

She went in and took a seat, being very quiet. He knew something was bothering her. She lay her head down on his desk and began to weep. He went around the desk and comforted her.

"What's the matter, Karen?"

"Mr. Brown, you are like family. How can I tell you what's happened?"

"You can always talk with me, Karen, no matter what."

"I have this job offer at KSOK. Are you going to get mad at me if I take it?" she sobbed.

"Karen, you'll always have a place here. We go back a long way." He then offered her his handkerchief. "Lenore and I will start watching more programs on KSOK. Now dry those eyes and don't you worry."

She put her arms around his waist, hugging him to her. He watched her leave, knowing the restaurant wouldn't be the same anymore.

CHAPTER 8

Monday afternoon, Karen began her first day at the station. She was to work on commercials for the station. The details came quickly for her, making it easy to learn the routine.

Several people were involved in this area. They would work on material the sales staff had previously sold. Imagination and new ideas were the mainstay of the commercials they were developing.

Karen's involvement helped them tremendously in the daily commercials. After a few weeks, all of them in the group came to see her potential. Fresh new ideas were always at her fingertips. She enjoyed her new job. Karen knew this was a career she would follow.

She would always miss everyone at Brown's, but KSOK took all her time now. Very often, they would work late on a project needed for a time slot.

Ruth didn't know Karen was working at KSOK. She and Ray were always gone. The months slipped quickly by, and now it was springtime at Grafton.

The first week of May, Karen was to see her counselor. She went into the office.

"I have an appointment with Mrs. Daily," Karen told the secretary.

The secretary said, "Mrs. Daily will see you now."

Karen wondered what Mrs. Daily wanted. Mrs. Daily motioned for Karen to take a seat.

"I have some very good news for you, Karen. You have been chosen as one of the students to receive a scholarship at Capitol City College. This will cover your last two years of college. Your grades are the highest of our graduating class, Karen. Congratulations!"

A lump formed in Karen's throat momentarily. Tears formed in her eyes as Mrs. Daily spoke to her. Mrs. Daily was pleased that someone quite deserving would receive the Dill scholarship award.

"I've studied so hard for my grades, plus working late hours at the station. It's so difficult."

She looked at the young woman in front of her. There was an inner beauty in those classic facial features Karen possessed. Mrs. Daily knew then that the committee had awarded the correct student.

"Thank you so very much, Mrs. Daily, I won't let Grafton College down."

This young woman had such an inner drive, Mrs. Daily thought, after Karen thanked her. Karen couldn't wait to tell Tiffany the good news.

They both were in a gay mood driving away. Karen told Tiffany her news. Tiffany had also received a scholarship. She too would be attending Capitol City College. Tiffany's degree was in counseling. She also received an offer to work in a family service office.

"Karen, let's go do something Friday night after graduation."

"Let's make it Saturday night. I've got some commercials to work on late."

Karen had arrived home after work, and Ray was home alone. She went into her room to change. She noticed Ray kept eyeing her. They made small conversations. Karen was on edge, not knowing what to do, being home alone with him. Her mother was out visiting a friend. Just as Karen opened the refrigerator, he tried to grab her. She turned away from him.

"Keep your hands off me, Ray."

Her mother came into the kitchen at this time. "Karen, don't worry about Ray. He won't hurt you."

With Ray's advances and Ruth's unbelieving attitude, matters only got worse during the summer.

While Ruth was gone one evening, Ray tried to pull Karen down on the couch. The following week, Karen took time off to have a locksmith repair her bedroom door lock. Ray continued making advances toward Karen. The only way to escape him was to lock herself in her room. After work one evening, she went over to visit with Molly.

"Why, honey, how are you? I haven't seen you in three months."

"Molly, can I get a sandwich and a glass of tea? I can't go home yet."

Molly fixed Karen a sandwich and a glass of tea. "What's going on, sweetheart?"

Karen looked pale, thin, and withdrawn. She began to speak in halting words.

She told Molly everything that was going on and how her mother accused her of making a play for Ray.

"Molly, he has tried to molest me. My mother won't believe me," she said, beginning to weep. "I missed you at my graduation."

Molly related that her sister had been ill in a nearby city. She had been there helping her.

"Mother didn't even come to my graduation."

Karen told Molly about her scholarship at Capitol City College, and that she would have to move there anyhow. They talked until quite late, then Karen went home.

She had changed into her pajamas and returned from the bathroom when Ray attacked her. He caught her by surprise, but she escaped into her room, locking the door behind her.

Ruth and Ray left for work early the next morning. Karen hadn't been able to talk to her mother about Ray's advances. She called in sick at KSOK.

Then she called Tiffany and told her everything. Tiffany called her office, taking the day off. Tiffany came over to pick her up. They stopped only long enough to buy a newspaper. The girls drove around for some time. They located a small apartment they could share. Karen felt better, knowing her best friend was with her.

They planned their moving out well. After several trips, both girls moved into their apartment. Karen had Tiffany take her to her mother's workplace.

It was lunch hour, and Ruth was outside smoking when Karen arrived.

"Hi, Mom. Have you had lunch?"

"What's going on, Karen?"

"Mom, we have to talk." Karen's voice was low and quiet as she began to talk.

"Mom, Ray has been trying to molest me on three different occasions while you were out of the house. He isn't going to stop unless you say something to him." She was nearly in tears by now.

"Karen, it's your fault, not Ray's."

"Mother, you are my only relative. I am a Christian. I'm telling you the truth. When have you not seen me go to church every Sunday? Mother, why can't you believe me? I'm your daughter. I can't remember the last time you ever hugged me. Don't you love me?" Karen was sobbing, taking in deep gulps of air, looking away from her mother.

"I'm moving into an apartment with Tiffany. I'll give you the address later. I'm a good girl, Mom. I work hard, go to church. You have to know I love you."

Her mother didn't reply or touch her, just watched as Karen left. Tiffany got out of her car and went over to Karen and hugged her. She helped Karen get seated in the car. Then she went over to Ruth and stood directly in front of her.

"You are losing someone special, Mrs. Spanek. I am always going to be Karen's friend."

Karen leaned against the dashboard of Tiffany's car, weeping, with her head in her arms. Her heart was broken as never before. She had no one except her friend Tiffany. Tiffany returned to the car, very upset at Ruth for what she had said to Karen.

"You've got me as a friend forever, Karen, count on it."

They drove to Molly's house. Molly met them at the door, asking them to come inside. The two girls sat on the sofa. Tiffany consoled Karen.

Then Tiffany told Molly everything that had happened at Ruth's place of employment. Molly sat down with them on the couch and hugged Karen.

"If you ever need me, honey, I'll be there for you."

Molly served them iced tea. Karen began to dry her eyes, then said, "You two are the only friends I have now. Tiffany, how can I ever repay you?"

They stayed only a short time, then left. Later, they walked into their apartment. The apartment was located in a quiet section of Stockton. It was neatly arranged, having room for all their belongings.

They unpacked all their clothes, then sat down at the kitchen table and planned the menus for the coming week. They decided to go to the grocery store and stock up. Karen was the more practical of the two at preparing meals.

Karen was now working full-time at the television station for the balance of the summer. She had been saving for an older car. She called Mr. Highsmith to ask for his advice.

They visited for some time, and then she asked if he would help her locate a drivable car in her price range. He told her he knew of one that was an older car but in good condition. He also told her he would take her over to see it.

Mr. Highsmith drove up and knocked on her apartment door.

"Mr. Highsmith, would you mind if I hugged you?"

The older man felt honored that she thought so much of him. He had known her for some time.

They got into his car and drove to the north side of Stockton, stopping in front of an older but neat house. They went to the door of the house and knocked. An older man came to the door, and Mr. Highsmith talked with him about the car in front of the house. It was a 1985 two-door Pontiac.

Karen had taken driving in high school. Ed guided her through the different switches on the dashboard. Everything worked properly. It didn't look fancy, but it was good transportation. Karen gave the man cash, counting it out on the table.

He gave her some tips about checking the various things of an automobile. Before driving off, Ed checked the water and oil in the engine. She got out of the car. He wondered what was wrong.

"Is everything all right, Karen?"

"Mr. Highsmith, I don't have a father, and I really needed you at this time to help me. I hope you didn't mind. Thank you so much for all your help. Just one more hug, and then I feel like I can go."

He watched her drive away, feeling like he had just watched a daughter drive out of his life. *If anyone should get a break, this one has it coming, Lord,* he thought.

Karen checked her driver's license before driving to the apartment. Tiffany drove to the apartment after work and saw an older Pontiac parked there.

"Whose car is that?" she asked herself.

Tiffany asked Karen whose car was parked outside. Karen told her that she had her friend, Mr. Highsmith, help her buy it.

"I thought I might as well get one, as I will need it next year at Capitol City."

The girls never had an argument. They got along as well as though they were sisters. Tiffany took Karen with her when she went home. The Prathers treated her just like one of the family. They would go with Molly to the thrift store and shop to buy items for their apartment.

Karen marveled that Tiffany never let anything get her down. She was always upbeat. They shared everything, often attending Karen's church together. One Sunday, Karen purchased a newspaper. Reading through the classifieds, an ad caught her eye. The ad was about a larger television station in Capitol City.

The position was in advertising commercials, preferably someone with experience. Karen was excited. This was a better position and would also help her locate there to finish college. She began to tell Tiffany about the ad.

Tiffany told her, "I'll take you over there to apply tomorrow. My folks are missing me."

They got up early and drove over to Capitol City for Karen's interview. Karen was dressed well for her interview at KJCH. They found the address, locating the station easily. Tiffany went in with her to wait. Karen carried an attractive brief case holding her resume and a large folder with ads she had worked on at her present station.

She went up to the receptionist and asked about the interview.

"I have an interview with Mr. Seigfried."

"He's been expecting you, Karen. Come this way."

She was led into an office where a man was sitting at a desk, obviously very busy. He had a slight build and thinning, sandy hair. He was in his early fifties. He rose, shaking her hand while motioning her to take a seat.

He took a few moments to look over her application before speaking. He looked up and smiled. "You're a very impressive young lady and apparently very bright." He asked her many questions about television commercials.

She explained that she had two more years to finish her degree at Capitol City College on a full scholarship. A smile never completely left his face.

Ray Seigfried liked her and was excited about her experience and scholastic background. Finally, he told her she was hired beginning in two weeks. She was to work in the afternoons during college. The rate of pay would be larger at KJCH.

August arrived, and Karen packed for her move to Capitol City. After the move, the changes would be enormous for Karen. Now she would be all alone.

Before leaving, Tiffany helped her find a small, efficient apartment. The girls moved out at the same time, packing their cars individually.

"Oh, Tiff, I'm going to miss you so."

"I'll drive over now and then to visit, you'll see."

The two friends hugged one last time. Karen had tears in her eyes. She drove away, feeling blue. Driving carefully, she arrived in front of her apartment and began to unload the car. Several trips later, she finished unloading everything. The landlady reminded Karen of Molly.

CHAPTER 9

Monday was her first day at KJCH. The work was much the same but with tighter schedules and more people.

Karen's experience helped her fit in, carrying more than her share of the workload. Her imagination and skills were recognized by all who worked with her. Karen applied for a job at a family style hamburger restaurant for weekend work.

The money would always come in handy. She always had a need for extra money as expenses never ceased. She budgeted her money as wisely as she could. There was never anything left over after payday.

The management was pleased with her work. There was a mixture of all ages working there. The weekends just seemed to run together.

One patron always sat in her work area. He would try to make small talk with her. By his clothing and manners, he looked like big money. Karen never felt at ease around him. He always drove a new Chrysler convertible.

Karen asked another waitress, "Jennifer, who is he anyway?"

"His name is Matt Dresser the third, and he is rich. He never seems to have a job or has to work but has lots of money to spend."

Matt always sat in Karen's work area. He was always trying to talk to her. Karen tried to ignore his advances. One evening after work, he stopped Karen as she was getting in her car to go home.

"Why are you ignoring me? I'm one of the nice guys."

She looked him over. He was wearing expensive clothes and a Rolex watch. His hands had a soft, manicured look. He had light brown hair and blue eyes with an effeminate appearance about him.

His approach had startled her and somehow was put on guard by him. She got into her car. He pushed her door shut. Unable to get away from him, she stopped to talk to him.

"Why don't I pick you up one evening this week? I'll take you to a nice place to eat. You do eat, don't you? What harm can there be in that?" he said, looking triumphant.

Searching for words, she said yes. Still in a panic, she answered, "I suppose for only a short time."

"Karen Spanek, where can I pick you up?" he asked. "What evening would be convenient for you?" he continued.

Not knowing what to say, she stammered, "Thursday evening, I guess. I cannot stay out late as I have a daytime job." She gave him her address.

"Well, I'll be there around seven o'clock."

Driving home, she became puzzled about the upcoming date for Thursday evening. Where did he get her name anyway? She was surprised to see Tiffany waiting for her to come home. They talked as only two friends could, filling each other in on everyday work. Then she told Tiffany about her upcoming date.

"Tiffany, should I go out with him?"

"Oh, everything will be all right. You and I are alike, we never date. Go ahead, you might have a good time."

The week dragged by for Karen. Tiffany came over to help her get ready. She pressed a pair of slacks and a blouse for the evening. Tiffany loaned her a pair of earrings and helped her with her hair.

Tiffany viewed her, saying, "You are a real knock-out, Karen. Have a good time."

They killed time visiting as Karen waited for Matt Dresser. A knock came on the door. She opened the door. He was wearing an expensive pair of slacks and shirt. She asked him inside. He stepped inside, introducing himself to Tiffany.

"I'm Matt Dresser," he said, holding out his hand to her.

Tiffany quickly looked him over. There was something about him that she couldn't quite put her finger on. This thought would linger on her mind throughout the evening.

"Have a good evening."

They left the apartment, going down the steps to his car. He opened the door of his convertible for her. It was almost dark as they drove away.

"Let me take you to Frazier's Steak House on the edge of town. Karen, where do you work during the regular workday?"

She related to him about her work at KJCH, how she got the job, and what her plans were for the future.

"Did you have good grades in high school?"

"I was valedictorian of my high school," she said proudly.

"I'll bet your parents are proud of your achievements."

"There's only my mother and myself now. My father died when I was eight years old. I was staying home, but my mother remarried. My stepfather wouldn't leave me alone, so I had to go out on my own."

He glanced over at her. She was a classic, a beautiful girl with dark hair, blue eyes, striking complexion, and a slender figure. Her clothes were clean, neat, and it suited her well. She was pretty in any league, he thought. After driving awhile, they arrived at Frazier's. Karen wasn't prepared to go in this place.

Music was being played by a small combo. Karen could smell the sickening odor of liquor and food in the air. Matt parked the car, then opened the door for her. He escorted her up the steps to the foyer inside. An older man approached Matt, greeting him. They made small talk out of Karen's range of hearing.

She became more apprehensive as she waited. More and more, she began to dread continuing this so-called date. She didn't feel comfortable at all.

A maitre d' seated them at a table near a window. A waiter later came to take any orders for bar drinks. Matt ordered a whiskey and soda. He asked Karen what she would like to drink.

"Tea will be fine for me," she said, declining any liquor.

The dining room had just begun to fill up. There was laughter and the clink of ice in the glasses of people drinking. Matt ordered another drink and still hadn't called for a waiter. Then he looked over at her and said, "You will like the food here." It was obvious he was becoming drunk. He left her to go to the bar and talk to some men gathered there. Finally, he returned from the bar.

"Let's order, I'm hungry now," he said.

A waiter brought them each a menu. Glancing at them, the waiter asked Karen what looked good to her. Not wanting to prolong the evening, she ordered a small steak, small salad, and a baked potato.

The waiter left, then returned with their salads. Karen wanted to tell him the food at Brown's was better than the food at Frazier's. While they were eating their salads, he kept looking in his shirt pocket. A short time later, the food arrived, and Matt appeared to sober up slightly.

Karen tried to appear upbeat, but it was difficult for her. By now, the club was in full swing. People were dancing and drinking, and the clatter of dishes added to the other noises. Matt ate slowly between drinks of whiskey and soda.

Finally, he finished eating. "Would you like dessert?" he asked.

Wishing to shorten the evening, she declined. Karen left to go to the ladies room. After returning, he was all smiles. He had ordered more tea for Karen. As she finished drinking it, he quickly signaled for a waiter and settled the bill with a handsome tip for the waiter.

"Are you ready to leave?"

She could see he was in a hurry to leave. All at once, she felt tired and relaxed. What could have made her feel this way? They went out to his car. Matt held her by the arm as they neared the car. He helped her into the seat. He closed the door after Karen sat down.

He went around the car, quickly driving away. Then he drove onto a main thoroughfare. She was just on the edge of consciousness. Then she realized what he had done. She had been given a date rape drug.

He is going to rape me, she thought. *This is only supposed to happen to someone else.*

Matt looked over at Karen. He was nearing the edge of town and turned into a country lane. He picked up her wrist, then dropped it. "This is number two almost too easy. They never know what has happened to them."

This is easier, he mused, *I don't have to go on several dates or make promises of marriage.*

The last one never turned him in to the police either. She was so dumb. In a dreamlike state, she could feel him touching her all over. She put her hands up to defend herself, but to no avail.

This man, whoever he is, was removing her clothing. He was violating her. Weeping and terror-stricken, she could only submit to him. It was finally over. Matt quickly dressed. It was getting late. Where could he leave her? An idea came to him. The city park. What a brilliant idea!

One side of the park was dark and only patrolled occasionally. He approached the park—no one in sight. He turned off his lights as he drove into the back of the park. The motor was left idling as he stopped. He ran around to lift Karen out of the car.

He laid her down on the freshly cut grass. She could somehow feel him drag her from the car. He threw her purse and clothing on top of her and drove away. She didn't stir despite the grass and trash she was lying on.

Would someone only help me? she thought. *Why did this man do this awful thing to me?*

It seemed as though time had stood still. Feeling and touching her body, Karen knew she was unclothed. Then she began to dress herself the best she could.

* * *

Walt Riebert awoke with a start from his concealed cardboard home in the park. It wasn't typical teenagers or the police patrol. He glanced at the dial of his luminous watch. The time was eleven o'clock. Was it a lovers' tryst that brought the new Chrysler into the park?

The lights were turned off. Keeping very still, he watched it come to a stop in a darkened area. Occasionally, lights flashing on it from a street light allowed him to see the proceedings.

The dome light afforded him a perfect view. The driver—tall, blond man—quickly opened the passenger door.

What is he doing? Walt wondered.

The young man pulled a nude young woman from the car. The driver began to throw articles of clothing and a purse near the body. Then he drove away.

The car stopped momentarily at the entrance of the park. There was no traffic visible, and the red car sped away in the night.

Walt was hesitant to get involved due to a previous charge of vagrancy. But he went to check on her anyway.

She appeared to be drugged but was breathing normally. Just as he finished checking her pulse, a police car emerged. Walt ran to his shelter. Karen became more awake.

She continued to put her clothes on. Partially dressed and weeping, she began to collect her thoughts. Karen felt very sick at her stomach. Her body ached from the attack and being pulled from the car.

Dave Glade and Herb Wilson were nearing the end of their watch as they checked the park. Dave drove slowly around to the back of the park. Nothing so far.

"Wait, Dave, someone is passed out over there."

"Call it in, Herb."

The officer had finished radioing in to the station. Then Karen heard the men's voices but could barely see the flashlight shining on her. They both walked over to her. She looked to be in her twenties. Karen was somewhat unconscious.

"Looks like she has been on dope. I don't smell any liquor on her. Why would she be partially undressed?"

The two officers lifted her up and put her on the back seat of the squad car. The officers finished radioing in their report to the station. They began driving to the station.

Now this terrible happening would be corrected, Karen thought.

She lay across the backseat in a stupor. The squad car came to a halt at the back of the station. She was forcibly hauled up some steps to a long desk.

A policeman there was booking some drunks, and several people charged with possession of drugs. Now it was Karen's turn to be interviewed and booked. The two policemen looked over their notes.

They charged her with being under the influence of drugs and several other charges. She tried to explain to them what had happened, but to no avail. They placed her in a cell with four other women. It was horrifying!

One girl, older than Karen, detached herself from the others and sat down beside Karen. "What are you in for, honey?"

"I'm charged with taking dope, but I have never drank or taken dope in my life. It started out as a date at a club called Frazier's. When I returned from the bathroom, I became groggy and finally passed out in the car. All I had to drink was iced tea."

"It sounds like they put rope in your tea, honey."

"What is this drug, rope, you are talking about?"

Just then, a jail matron came to the cell. The time was one o'clock.

"Karen Spanek, you can make a phone call if you wish."

The matron then opened the cell door for Karen, telling her which phone she could use. The only one she knew to call was Tiffany. After three rings, a sleepy voice came on the line. Tiffany could hear someone weeping on the phone.

"Hello. Who is this?"

"It's Karen. I'm in jail at the police station. Please come and help me Tiffany, I need you," Karen sobbed.

"I'll be down as quickly as I can." Tiffany dressed hurriedly, then left in her car. *What has happened to Karen,* she wondered. Moment later, she arrived at the police station.

She went to the booking sergeant on duty and inquired about Karen S. Spanek. Tiffany asked what Karen had been charged with.

"She had been charged with taking dope, outraging public decency, and indecent exposure."

Tiffany was incensed at the charges of her friend who worked hard and went to church every Sunday of her life. Something was wrong here. She signed for Karen's release. The matron on duty left and then returned with a disheveled Karen.

CHAPTER 10

Karen began to weep and hugged Tiffany, not wanting to let go of her. Tiffany led a crying Karen to a nearby bench.

"Karen, what in the world happened to you? Tell me all about it."

Karen began at the beginning and concluded with the part of waking up in the park unclothed.

"All I did was go on a date. I didn't want to go on, and now look at me."

Karen finished telling everything she knew. Tiffany was beginning to get red in the face. She was so mad. Her eyes sparkled with anger.

"He's not going to get away with this. First things first, we'll go see a detective before anything else."

Tiffany went over to the sergeant and asked to see a detective. He told them which detective was on duty, and what the room number was. They went into the room and met with detective Tim Downs.

Tiffany told him Karen wanted to charge Matt Dresser III with the rape of her friend, Karen Spanek. He listened attentively to all the facts.

"For starters, she should have been taken to a local hospital for examination. We may have lost some valuable evidence. Your case will be weak at best as it will only be your word against his. I'll do everything I can to help your case. Many times, it's 'she said' and 'he said' type of case."

They left his office and went back into the booking area. Tiffany said, "We are going to call an organization I'm familiar with which can help you. It's called Call Rape."

They waited for some time until a slightly built gray haired woman in her fifties arrived. It was now 2:00 a.m. The sergeant greeted Mrs. Irene Adkins.

Then she turned her attention to the girls before her. Tiffany identified herself to Mrs. Adkins. She took Karen's hand in hers. She saw a beautiful, distraught young woman sitting on the bench before her.

Irene asked Karen to tell her everything that had happened. While she told her story, Karen wiped tears from her eyes.

"I'm going to help you in more ways than one, but first, we must go to the hospital for an examination. This is the first thing we must do. I'll meet you over at the hospital."

Tiffany and Karen walked to the car and drove to the designated hospital. The staff there asked Karen to go into an examination room. Less than an hour later, the exam was over. Mrs. Adkins talked some more to Karen, giving her a business card. She set up an appointment for Karen at a later time.

"I know what you're going through as my daughter was date raped also. That's why I'm in this program. I'm on your side, and I'm going to help you in any way I can, Karen. Bye for now, and I will see you at a later time."

Tiffany and Karen left the hospital. Tiffany put her arm around Karen's waist as they walked to the car. They got into the car and drove to Karen's apartment. Karen began to murmur.

"My life is ruined now. I go to church, work hard, and try to be a good person. What am I going to do now?"

"Karen, I'm your friend, and I'll stand by you in this time of trouble because that's what friends are supposed to do."

Karen was quiet as they drove home. She slept fitfully the rest of the night. Going to work the next day was an ordeal for her, but somehow, she got through the day. She appeared withdrawn, not commenting on the team's efforts.

Karen had just arrived home when a man identified as a detective met her at the door. He showed her his identification and badge. He took every detail in a report. Karen informed him of her church, giving him her pastor's name as a character reference.

"I don't drink and have never drank or taken any manner of drugs. I only know I passed out after I returned from the bathroom at the club called Frazier's. I remember he told me that he had ordered me another glass of tea before I had returned to the table. After drinking the tea, we left the club."

Karen was trying to put the rape behind her. Work was the one thing that helped her get through it all. The case against Matt Dresser was a weak one at best. The district attorney informed her that without good solid evidence, it was useless to file a case.

One morning after the third week, Karen felt nauseated and sick at her stomach. She couldn't keep any food down. *What could I have eaten?* she thought.

This began to happen every morning. She knew then she was pregnant.

Karen sat at the kitchen table, laying her head in her arms. Tears formed in her eyes. Surely, God wouldn't punish her for this. She wished to have a family only after marriage, not like this.

Questions formed in her mind. *I am barely surviving now. What must I do now?* Perhaps Mrs. Adkins would have her an idea where to start? Karen knew she couldn't get by all this alone. She searched in her purse for Mrs. Adkin's card.

In a more affluent section of Capitol City, Clarissa Dresser smiled as she greeted her son Mathew.

"Mathew dear, did you have a date Friday?"

"Mother, that was three weeks ago."

"Well, how did it go son? Was she anyone your mother should meet?"

"Mother, she has been after me to ask her out on a date, so I took her out that one time."

"Matt, you need to find someone you can settle down with. Don't get into trouble son, our good name, you know."

Just then, the doorbell rang. Clarissa went to the door. A man identified himself as Tim Downs of the Capitol City police.

"Officer, is this about the policemen's ball tickets?"

"No. Does a Mathew Dresser live here?"

"What's this about, Officer, a traffic ticket my son hasn't paid? I'll call my son, and we'll get this settled."

"I have several questions for a Matthew Dresser III. I must see him alone."

She escorted the detective into the study. The room was filled with expensive books and furniture. Matt joined him in the study. Tim Downs sized up the young man in front of him. *Too much money and time on his hands,* he thought.

Matt tried to look calm and nonchalant, not breaking a sweat. The detective asked him questions pertinent to Karen's case. Tim Downs concluded by putting his notebook in his pocket.

"What are these questions in regard to, Officer?"

"A young woman named Karen Spanek has filed charges against you. The charges are rape and using a drug called rohypnol, or date rape drug. Another name we go by is rope."

"Are there anymore questions? I'm not going to be questioned anymore without my lawyer present."

"That's all the questions I have for now."

Matt escorted the detective to the front door. His mother waited until he the shut the door before speaking.

"What's this all about, Matt?"

"Nothing, Mother, that girl told the police I made an improper advances on her. Besides, she was drinking heavily before we ever left Frazier's."

"Matt, you are going to work in one of my factory offices. You need to begin doing regular work and keeping regular hours."

Matt watched his mother leave the room. He smiled. *She will soon forget this, knowing her social schedule,* Matt mused.

Clarissa went into her office and closed the door. *He is weak, but I did the best I could alone.* What more could she have done for her son? He had been disciplined very little throughout his life.

She opened the first drawer on her left. She pulled out a leather bound address book from it. Thumbing through it, she stopped at the "R's." She hurriedly dialed Ben Ryerson's number.

"Ryerson's Detective Agency. How may I help you?"

"My name is Clarissa Dresser. I must speak with Ben please."

Ben Ryerson took the call. He was a slightly balding man in his early fifties. His sandy hair was sprinkled with gray. His face looked as though he had spent too many hours in the ring. But this very demeanor had fooled men much younger. Ben was a retired Capitol City Police Department detective.

"Ben, this is Clarissa Dresser."

"Clarissa, what can I do for you?"

"Ben, a Capitol City detective came to my house and questioned my son this morning. Can you find out what this is all about?"

"I'll call in some markers and get some answers."

"Bill me here at the house marked 'Private' please. I'll pay you by return mail."

He hung up the phone. This was one of many times that he had been called throughout the past years to help get her son out of different problems. Would this problem be the one that Matt couldn't get out of?

Clarissa was one of his best clients. She had used him to check on her friends, social, and otherwise. Everyone was but a game for her. She had an inquiring mind. He laughed.

Then Clarissa turned to the "H's" in her address book. Donavon Henry was known as the premier defense attorney in several states. Clarissa cared little about his exorbitant fees. She dialed a downtown Capitol City number.

"Donavon Henry's Law Office. How may I help you?"

"My name is Clarissa Dresser. I must speak with Donavon please."

"Hi, Clarissa, how may I help you?"

His cultured voice was smooth and articulate. A man in his early forties who commanded attention from everyone. He was very popular after a successful college football career.

Donavon's stock in trade was his magnetic personality. His ability to draw facts and truth out of his clients made him such a successful lawyer.

His thoughts turned to previous calls by Clarissa Dresser. The calls were often about clearing her son of some type of charges. Matt had too much free time, and no discipline like sports could give him.

"A Capitol City detective came to the house to ask Matthew some questions. You have worked with the Ryerson detective agency before, haven't you?"

"Call Ben. But first, give him a chance to look into what the charges are."

"Okay."

"I'll call you after I find out what I'm dealing with, Clarissa."

She hung up the phone, then looked at a photograph on her desk. A young man smiled at her. Matthew Dresser was killed in an automobile accident at the age of thirty eight. She was left with a little baby to raise all alone. He was off on one of his empire building ventures.

Clarissa had been running the entire company alone since then, by sheer grit and determination. She had never remarried for fear of losing another loved one. Would fate take her only son away?

A month had passed since Karen had been booked. The district attorney had her meet him at his office. He went over her case with her, stating that her case was a weak one. Matt had stated that she had become inebriated on the night in question. Also, that he had taken her directly home after dinner.

She thanked the district attorney for his time. He told her he would keep the case open. The investigation showed that Matt had other charges filed against him before.

Karen felt sad and spiritually down as she drove home after meeting with the district attorney. She felt a sharp twinge as she parked. She let herself into the apartment. She took Mrs. Adkins's card from her purse.

Her friend Tiffany was on her way over to visit Karen. Driving near the apartment house, she saw a light on in Karen's apartment window. Karen's car was parked out front. She parked her car and let herself in with her key.

Karen was sitting at the kitchen table with her head down on folded arms. Tiffany put her handbag down on the couch and went over to Karen. She touched Karen on the shoulder.

"What's the matter, honey?"

Karen lifted her head. There were tears gathering in those blue eyes. "Oh, Tiffany, I'm pregnant." Karen looked blank. "I'm not having an abortion. My God wouldn't want me to."

"You're a fighter, Karen, and will make a great mother. That little baby will be the luckiest child in the whole world."

"We'll call Mrs. Adkins and get some help through her. There are some tremendous programs out there for you."

Tiffany dialed the number on the card. A woman answered the telephone. It was Mrs. Adkins. Tiffany identified herself, mentioning she was calling for Karen Spanek. Mrs. Adkins agreed to meet them at Karen's apartment.

An hour later, there was a knock on the door. It was Mrs. Adkins.

"Can we just sit at the kitchen table?" she asked.

Before writing down any information, she took Karen by the hand, saying, "You and I will get through this together."

She asked Karen· to tell her story from the beginning. Karen concluded, with where the rape case stood at this time.

"I just returned from the district attorney's office. He said my case was a weak one at best. I am very sure that I'm pregnant. The detective said he agreed with me that I was drugged by Matt Dresser. The drug used on me was a drug called rohypnol."

Mrs. Adkins listened to Karen complete her story. She outlined the programs available to Karen. She then removed various forms from her briefcase for Karen to fill out.

These could help her get the proper medical help she would need during her pregnancy. She informed Karen if she needed anymore help to call her. Then Mrs. Adkins left.

Tiffany helped Karen complete all five of the forms Mrs. Adkins had left. The forms were very detailed. They told what doctor and agency she would be associated with.

It would be an agency of Harris County Health Department headquarters in Capitol City. This department would provide assistance during her pregnancy, such as a doctor, prenatal care, and the hospital involved.

After Tiffany left, Karen sat down, with her head in her hands, and wondered, "Will I be able to get through all this? Will prayers and help from my only friend get me through it?"

The next morning, Karen went in to see her boss, Mr. Siegfried.

"What can I help you with this morning, Karen?"

"Mr. Siegfried, I'd like to keep our conversation just between the two of us."

CHAPTER 11

Karen began very slowly, nearly in tears. She fumbled with her words, speaking haltingly. She told him the complete story. When she finished, he came around the desk to hug her.

"What has happened to you is horrible. I can imagine that might happen to anyone. You poor child, we are all family here. I am glad you have told me. I'll help you in any way that I can. My lips are sealed. I'm sure in the months to come, you will need time off now and then."

"Thank you, Mr. Siegfried. I'm going to have the baby, not an abortion."

He looked at the beautiful young woman in front of him. He thought, *Why is it always the least of these that carry the largest burdens?* He then pulled a handkerchief from his pocket and offered it to Karen. She thanked him quietly for his understanding and left.

Before leaving for work the next morning, Karen went through the brochure left by Mrs. Adkins. Everything concerning her pregnancy was explained. The doctor, prenatal checkups, and even baby food would be provided.

The hospital would be the Good Samaritan Hospital in Capitol City. All of these programs were part of the Harris County Health Department. They were funded by the Capitol City United Way.

Karen left work for her first appointment. She drove to the clinic. A director, Mrs. Larson, checked her forms. She was assigned to a Dr. Michaels. Her first appointment was set up for that very afternoon. His offices were in the same building. She went to room 265. A nurse there took the forms Karen held in her hands. She was asked to take a seat.

The doctor who entered the waiting room had dark hair, dark eyes with a swarthy complexion. He smiled as he introduced himself.

"Now, Karen, you must relax. From now on, you and your baby will come first with me. Let's go into the exam room and get started."

She felt at ease with this kindly man. After the exam was over, he talked with her about the proper diet, vitamins, proper rest, and exercise. He asked her about any medicine she was taking at the present time.

He smiled as he discussed the various food groups involved and dwelt on nutrition. Before she left the exam room, he said, "You're young and healthy and will have a fine baby. See you in two weeks."

She left his office with booklets about baby foods, such as Enfamil, and eating timetables. Karen's spirits lifted somewhat as she drove home.

"I must call Molly," she vowed. Karen parked, then went into her apartment. She put on a kettle for some tea before calling Molly.

She dialed Molly's number and heard a familiar voice answer the phone. It was Molly.

"Oh, honey, I've had you in my mind for the last two weeks."

Karen hesitated but felt compelled to tell this one who was like a mother to her. "Molly, I have some bad news to tell you."

She heard Molly breathe a deep sigh. Karen told her everything about the rape, and that she was going to keep the baby.

"Oh, my baby," Molly repeated. "I'll come over tomorrow, and we will visit."

Karen was delighted that she would see Molly soon. Midmorning on Saturday, there was a knock on the door.

It was Molly. Karen rushed into her arms and burst into tears. Molly consoled her. Karen prepared tea for them. They visited for an hour without stopping. Karen told Molly her baby was due in the month of May. Molly filled Karen in on what was happening with her mother and Ray Gould.

"They have been drinking and fighting over there, but I never see much of them though."

When Molly was leaving that afternoon, she said, "We'll go shopping for some baby clothes, stroller, and a baby bed. I am going to be a stand-in grandmother."

After Molly left to go home, Karen dressed for work at the hamburger place. She would work as long as she was able. *I can use every dime from now on,* she thought.

Karen continued to work two jobs after her ordeal. She never mentioned to anyone what a nightmare it had been for her. The last year at Grafton Junior College had begun. She made arrangements around her classes while working at the television station.

Two months had passed since the incident, and Karen felt she must talk with her school counselor. The truth was the only route to take, she decided.

It was on a Wednesday when she had an appointment after classes with Mrs. Nancy Olson. Mrs. Olson, a woman in her late forties, asked Karen into her office and closed the door behind them.

"What may I help you with, Karen?"

"Can this be just between you and me?"

"Counselors are to keep all things between them and their students confidential."

Karen began to weep, unable to speak. Mrs. Olson went around the desk to comfort her and offered her a tissue. Finally, Karen composed herself enough t talk.

"Mrs. Olson I was date raped at the end of the summer," she began. "I'm alone now because my stepfather tried to molest me. My mother sided with him, and I had to leave home."

Mrs. Olson could see the terrible burden this young girl was carrying alone. Karen continued, "Mrs. Olson, all my life I've gone to church and worked ever since I can remember. My goal is to get a good education. Will this affect my scholarship?"

Mrs. Olson sat back down at her desk. She began to read through Karen's transcript and background in a folder she was holding. "Karen, you are one of the finest students we have ever had here at Grafton. You have made As in all your classes."

She looked directly at Karen and assured her about her academic standing. "Come in any time you feel like talking. I'll help you in any way I can, Karen."

Saturday was a pretty fall day when Molly arrived. Tiffany had been there earlier but had to leave for work.

"Molly, why me?"

"We never know why these things happen to good people, honey," Molly insisted. "Well, let's go shopping for all the things you will need for the baby. You will also need some maternity clothes."

Karen never asked Molly how her mother was doing. What difference would it make anyway. They left in Molly's car to go to a shopping mall on the edge of town. They chatted like two magpies the entire two hours they were gone. Molly purchased all the things Karen would need until the baby's arrival.

After lunch, they drove back to Karen's apartment. Before Molly drove away, Karen kissed her on the cheek, saying, "Whatever would I do without you, Molly?"

Molly dabbed at her eyes, saying, "Call me now, little one, if you ever need me."

Karen stood at the curb, watching until Molly had driven out of sight. She reluctantly went back up to her apartment. The loneliness was difficult to deal with.

Karen's doctor appointments were every other Thursday. It was November and time for another appointment. Perhaps she would be able to find out if the baby was to be a boy or a girl this time.

Thursday afternoon, she went into Dr. Michael's office. The nurse checked her files.

"You are Karen Spanek, aren't you? Let's get you ready. Go into room number three."

Karen went into the room and changed, waiting quietly for the doctor. Soon the door opened, and he entered.

"Karen, how have you been feeling? Have you been taking your vitamins and watching what you eat? Your next visit will be in December."

"Yes, Doctor, I am feeling fine. I am also taking my vitamins as you instructed. Will I get to find out today what my baby's sex will be?"

He smiled as he wrote on her medical chart. He left her to finish dressing. Karen was feeling tired with the college classes and working at the television studio in the afternoon. There were class assignments and papers to prepare.

Around midnight, Karen went to bed, quite exhausted. She knew she would have to quit her job at the hamburger place. The fast pace was just too much for her. The manager told her she had a job anytime she wished to return.

This would allow more time to study and rest. Now her feet began to swell. Her fellow workers at the station helped her in every way they could. One of the girls gave a baby shower for her. Karen couldn't believe people could be so nice.

This was Friday, and she would have no classes during Thanksgiving. She felt so blue as she let herself in the apartment after work. Saturday morning, there was a knock on her door. She hastily donned a bathrobe, then opened the door.

She stared at a huge box in front of the door. Two hands held onto to it at the top. Then a voice sounded from behind it. Who else but her brassy blond friend, Tiffany Prather.

"Hi, Tiffany, so good to see you. What in the world do you have in that box?"

"Well, can't an aunt buy your little one a baby bed? This baby better be a girl because I spoil girls better than I do boys. Now don't cry on me as you'll get me to crying too."

"Oh, Tiffany, you shouldn't have, but thank you so much."

Karen wasn't looking at a tall, blue-eyed, brash, outgoing person, but she was looking at an angel. She thought, *I have two friends, and many people never have one close friend.*

"Look, kid, the cheer-up committee is here. Pack up your duds and let's go. Get aboard the Prather-bound special."

"Tiffany, could we have a cup of coffee before we go? I'm starved."

Karen put on a pot of coffee, then they sat down at the table and caught up on each other's activities.

"Now, Karen, if I don't come home with you soon, I'll have to find myself a room. Mama can't wait for you to get there. You are her little chick."

An hour later, Tiffany placed Karen's suitcase and book bag in the trunk of her car.

"Karen, did you get everything? I'm not bringing you back until the holidays are over."

Karen was all smiles as her friend took over. Tiffany had greatly lifted her spirits. Tiffany quickly drove the miles to her home in Stanton. She drove up in the driveway of a large, ranch style house. It was well landscaped, looking much like a large doll house with everything painted and in its place.

Just then, Beverly Prather came out of the house. She was a big, raw-boned woman with freckles and big blue eyes. Her smile would melt any heart. Karen could feel two big arms go around her. She felt a kiss on her cheek.

Karen could feel tears come into her eyes. No one had ever hugged her quite like that, and she could feel herself let go. She sobbed softly.

"Oh, sweetheart, you are home now. Come inside. I didn't mean to upset you. You are to rest while you're here."

"Thank you so much for having me."

Beverly Prather walked by her side, and they went into the house. She smoothed Karen's hair back while reaching for a tissue.

"You are all Tiffany talks about. She thinks you can almost walk on water. Get settled, then come into the kitchen, and let's visit."

After a short time, Karen went into the kitchen with Tiffany. The kitchen was bright and sparkled. Beverly poured Karen and Tiffany glasses of tea. Karen could see love in the family living here. Presently, Harold Prather came into the kitchen.

"Kitten, who is the lovely little bird in our kitchen?"

"It's my very best friend, Karen Spanek. Give her one of your famous hugs."

Harold was a big-framed man with an easy smile, a rugged-looking man. Karen rose to shake his hand and was immediately held and hugged.

They all sat down at the kitchen table and began to talk. Karen enjoyed this immensely, never having been part of a real family.

"Tiffany, did you rent some movies?" her mother asked.

"Yes, enough for the rest of the week anyway. But first, I want to find out if Karen would like to rest awhile."

"Tiffany, I need to go over some classwork first," Karen replied.

"I have an extra desk in my room you can use. Karen was valedictorian at her high school. She makes straight As, Mom."

The girls went into Tiffany's room to study. They studied for well over an hour. Karen's eyelids became heavy. She couldn't stay awake.

"Karen, lie down and rest for a while."

Her friend helped her to the bed. It was so quiet and peaceful she fell asleep quickly. What seemed like hours later, she awoke with a start. What was everyone doing? Tiffany came into the room.

"You're awake. Would you like to walk around the neighborhood?"

They put on light jackets as there was a chill in the air. Beverly watched them go outside. The house was surrounded with flowerbeds. It was late afternoon. The trees flashed their kaleidoscope of colors as they walked.

Tiffany talked about her classes and why she had taken psychology. She talked about working with the State Department of Health. She discussed a few of the many cases she had worked with. She finished by saying, "It's always the children who pay a heavy price in most of them it seems."

Karen talked about the commercials she had help develop. Tiffany could see how intelligent Karen was, knowing Karen was in the correct profession.

They had completed a mile and began reversing their route. Soon they were back home. Beverly called to them as they entered the house.

"Hi, girls, supper will be ready soon."

They all sat down to a well-prepared meal. Karen enjoyed the atmosphere. There was small talk for everyone to relate to. They joined hands while Harold said a lovely prayer. For Karen, the clink of dishes and the good food made the meal even more enjoyable.

"Now, Mrs. Prather, it is Tiffany's and my turn to do the dishes. I grew up working in kitchens. Let us do this."

CHAPTER 12

"Karen, please call me Beverly. I think Tiffany needs more lessons of domesticity."

Tiffany and Karen took over. Clearly, Karen was in her element. Tiffany was surprised at how well Karen worked. They hung up their aprons after having cleaned the kitchen, and all the dishes were put away.

They all gathered in the living room to watch a movie. The movie was a popular one. It was nearing ten o'clock when it was over. Everyone headed for their bedrooms. Tiffany turned on a television set in her bedroom for a weather report.

The weather was to turn colder. Both girls put on their pajamas before watching Jay Leno. The television was then turned off. The days passed quickly for Karen. She felt in heaven, staying with this wonderful family. They played board games of every kind. Tomorrow would be Thanksgiving.

The girls slept late. The aroma of baking turkey and pumpkin pies filled the air. Beverly was busy in the kitchen, singing an old familiar church hymn as she worked.

Karen's mind turned to her church where she had spent so many Sundays. "I must make an appointment with Reverend Wilcox. I must ask him to pray for me and have God with me." Her thoughts were interrupted by Tiffany jumping out of bed.

"Let's go into the kitchen and see what Mom is doing. Mama, we just wanted to see what all you are preparing. We will get dressed and help you."

Tiffany and Karen helped in many ways. They set the table. It looked beautiful with Beverly's best china and tableware. Just then, there was a knock on the door. Tiffany answered, hugging an older couple. It was her aunt Mazie and uncle Grant.

They hugged each other, greeting Beverly, Karen, and Harold. Tiffany introduced Karen to them. The men talked of friends, work, and football.

"This is my very best friend, Karen Spanek. We go to college together."

They saw a beautiful young woman with dark raven hair and haunting blue eyes. Finally, the meal was ready with Mazie and Beverly setting the last dishes of food on the table.

They all took their places around the table. They then joined hands, bowing their heads. Harold said a prayer of grace. A simple one, but it was touching to hear. Everyone answered with an amen when he finished.

Beverly was delighted that her guests had hearty appetites. Not much was left of the bounteous meal. After dinner, Mazie and Beverly refused any help from Karen or Tiffany. The girls went to watch the football game with the men.

Evening spread its mantle of darkness around the neighborhood. Tiffany kidded and cut up with her uncle. Grant asked Tiffany if she would give him half-price for her sessions when she became a psychologist.

Tiffany laughed as she answered, "I'd probably charge you double, Uncle Grant."

Tiffany's uncle Grant asked Karen what type of work she did. Karen told him she worked for a television station in Stanton.

She began to explain how they created commercials, how they were used, and how they were displayed. He was certainly impressed by Karen. Much later in the evening, Tiffany's uncle and aunt left to go home.

Karen knew she should return home also. They next day, Friday, Karen packed to go home. She wished to get home early enough to visit with her pastor.

She waited at the front door for Tiffany to take her back home. Beverly and Harold both hugged her and told her to come back soon.

"Thank you for asking me for Thanksgiving holiday. I enjoyed it so much."

"You're most welcome, honey. Come visit us whenever you can."

They got into Tiffany's car, waving as they drove away. Shortly, Karen was back in her apartment. She phoned Reverend Wilcox. He was happy to hear from her.

"Hello, Karen, I've been missing one of the most faithful of my flock. How can I help you?"

"May I come to your study to see you privately?"

"You surely may. This is a very appropriate time."

Karen drove to the parking lot near the church office. She went in the side door of the church. Reverend James Wilcox's study door was open, waiting for her. No one else was in the church at that time.

He arose, taking her hands in his. They both sat down. He could see tears forming in her eyes. She began to weep. He went around his desk to comfort her, "You, God, and I are the only ones here, Karen. Tell me what is in your heart."

Karen began with her stepfather's attempt to molest her. How her mother wouldn't believe her. She related how she was living alone in Capitol City. She finished by telling him how she had been date raped. Reverend Wilcox could understand the burden Karen was carrying.

"I'm not having an abortion, Pastor. I know God will help me in this trial. I so wanted to see you and talk with you about all this."

"Karen, you've been a member since the age of eight. Almost always, you've been alone as you attended services. Now you've grown up, but you are not alone. We, as your church, are to help one another. That's God's way. Let me say a prayer with you now."

He stood while holding her hands in his. James Wilcox drew from his soul an eloquent, impassioned prayer. Then he went around to his desk, hunting for an envelope.

What could he be doing? Karen questioned.

He then withdrew his billfold from his hip pocket and placed all the money from it into the envelope. He handed the envelope to Karen. She tried to decline the gift.

"Take this, little one, and your church will respond in a Christian manner soon."

She got up to leave and hugged him again after promising to attend church very soon. Karen felt a huge weight rise from her shoulders as she drove home.

In another area of Stanton, a woman was sitting alone at her kitchen table. Ruth was questioning why her husband wasn't there with her.

"Why is Ray working so much overtime lately?" Ruth questioned. She had been waiting for him to return home for the supper she had prepared earlier. He explained that the company had a huge workload to finish in just a short time.

Thanksgiving had been a mess for Ruth. Ray invited a few of his old drinking buddies over. She had cooked from early morning to late afternoon. They just drank heavily and trashed her kitchen. Not one of them had thanked her for the dinner.

Not one had lifted a hand to help. Then after eating, they all took off to go to Bill's bar for more partying. She was angry at Ray for asking them without her knowledge.

Ruth never for one moment gave any thought of her daughter, Karen. She wondered what she should get Ray for Christmas. Ruth knew Christmas was only a short time away.

"I'm certainly not going to cook a big dinner for all his drinking cronies!"

In another part of town, a woman waited in her apartment. She hoped her new boyfriend would be in town, from his cross-country truck driving.

There was a knock on the door. Sally Hinds became excited as she opened the door.

"I can only stay three hours as I have a run later tonight out of state."

Ray stayed as long as he could, then left. She was another sucker, Ray thought as he hugged and kissed her good-bye. He told women what they wanted to hear. Ray had been playing the field for years. Marriage vows were for fools.

Finally, at nine thirty, Ray returned. Ruth heated the supper she had prepared hours ago. She believed his story about working late. Their marriage was a solid one, and no woman could steal her man.

* * *

Tiffany invited Karen home for the Christmas holidays. The two spent Christmas studying for semester finals. With work and a full college class schedule, Karen was exhausted all the time.

Tiffany amazed her, constantly being upbeat. Now they were in the spring semester. She had to struggle to maintain her grades. The weather was changing into blustery April showers.

Karen had difficulty walking and was wearing large maternity dresses now. Her back ached constantly with work and the baby's growing movements.

Karen had been taking the prescribed vitamins and maintaining a proper diet. On her last visit with Dr. Michaels, Karen learned her baby was to be a girl. He told her it was due to be born the last of May. Tiffany was like a mother hen, scolding her while helping.

May began with pretty sunny days. Karen was moving slower and more carefully now. The semester was almost over. The grades had now been posted. Karen missed being valedictorian by two points.

In one class, Karen received a note to see Mrs. Olson, her counselor.

"What could this meeting be about?" she questioned. She walked slowly to the administration building.

Thank heaven it wasn't on the second floor as none of the buildings had elevators.

The secretary took her name as she arrived at Mrs. Olson's office. She was escorted in immediately. Mrs. Olson was busy talking on the telephone, then hung up.

"How are you, Karen?" she asked, smiling. She asked Karen about her classes, work, and her physical well-being. "I'm excited about what I just heard on the telephone, Karen," Nancy Olson explained. "You are the recipient of a two-year scholarship at Capitol City University."

Karen was stunned to hear such news. "God was surely on His throne," were the words on her tongue. "Mrs. Olson, bless you, bless you. How can I ever thank you?" Karen said quietly.

"You have earned it the old-fashioned way—hard work, dear. When is your baby due?"

"The last of this month—graduation."

"We'll mail you your diploma. Sorry you will miss this important time."

Karen could hardly wait to get home and tell Tiffany. Tiffany arrived at the apartment, noting the smile on Karen's face.

Why was her best friend smiling like that? Tiffany thought. "Okay. Why are you looking like a cat with a feather in its mouth?"

"Guess who got a two-year scholarship to Capitol City University?"

"Congratulations, Karen, you deserve it. I heard on campus that you missed valedictorian by two points."

Tiffany placed her hand on Karen's stomach, saying, "Paige, you've got one smart mama."

They celebrated by fixing hamburgers on the grill for supper. It was becoming more difficult for Karen to get around easily. Thank heaven classes were over.

It was not the last week in May yet. She was unusually tired after getting home from work at KJCH. Karen went to bed earlier than usual.

She awoke early, feeling quite ill all at once. The baby had kicked from time to time, making any rest impossible. In all this pain, Karen noted the closeness of the labor pains.

She called in sick at the station. She got up from the bed with difficulty. She then called Dr. Michael's office to say she was on her way to the Good Samaritan Hospital. Then she pulled a small suitcase out of the closet, collected her purse, and went outside to her car. Before leaving the apartment, she left a short note for Tiffany.

In tremendous pain, she opened the car door, placing the small suitcase behind the driver's seat. Ironic as the thought could be, Karen's mind was on her mother at that moment.

Why couldn't she be here with me at the most this important moment of my life? Why couldn't her mother believe her about Ray Gould's intentions? These thoughts made her feel sad as she drove.

Karen drove slowly and carefully to the central part of Stanton. She drove into the parking lot at the hospital and parked her car. She opened the car door and paused as she reached for the small suitcase there. She began walking toward the emergency room.

Only fifty feet more and she would reach the door. What was happening? Her legs wouldn't function, and she couldn't go on. Karen knew she was about to pass out and couldn't help herself. Darkness came over her, then oblivion. Unknown to her, two strong hands caught her as she began to fall. It was a young intern working at the hospital.

"Bring a wheel chair out here!" he shouted to the emergency group inside.

"Must get to the hospital," were her last words.

Quite some time later, she awoke with an older woman holding her by the hand. The lady was smiling down at her. The smells of the hospital struck her senses. She felt the gown around her body as she lay there. Her eyes fluttered open. She heard a voice speaking to someone nearby.

"We have all the information on the chart ready for you, Doctor."

Her bed was being wheeled away to another part of the hospital. She was now surrounded by nurses and Dr. Michael.

He said, "Young lady, it looks as though it's time for you to become a mother."

Following all their instructions, amid screams and immense pain, Karen could hear the cry of a baby. They checked the baby over, wrapped the tiny baby in a blanket, and handed her to Karen.

Tears came into her eyes as she held the baby in her arms. *She's mine, and no one will ever hurt her,* Karen thought. The glow of love was there at that moment of God's magic.

This was the same love and closeness felt by many mothers, before her down through the ages. The tiny baby moved in her arms. Though very tired, nothing could stop the elation she felt at this time.

Arriving home from work, Tiffany looked for Karen, then spied the note on the kitchen table. She picked up her purse and keys and returned to her car. She drove as fast as she could near the speed limit, parking in the visitor's lot.

Couldn't someone share this moment with me? Karen thought.

Tiffany found Karen's room quickly. She looked in the room and at the young woman lying there, with her face so white and drawn, holding a tiny baby. Karen didn't know her friend was there. Tiffany walked quietly up to the bed, wanting to be certain it was her friend. Tears ran down Tiffany's face.

Karen opened her eyes and looked up at her. "Oh, thanks for being here for me today."

"Karen, I came as soon as I could. Let Aunt Tiffany look at you, Paige."

Karen pulled the blanket away from Paige's face to show Tiffany her baby. *My best friend is with me now, and that is good enough for me,* Karen thought. Tiffany had to hold the little girl. Karen let Tiffany take the baby from her arms.

"You have two people who love you very much, little one. I'll call Molly and your pastor for you."

A nurse came into the room to take the baby back to the nursery. She told Karen she would have to rest now. Tiffany leaned over to kiss Karen on the forehead.

"I'll be back later, sweetie."

Late in the afternoon, Karen awoke from a nap. Earlier, she got to bottle-feed Paige for the first time. Just then, a nurse brought a beautiful potted plant from Tiffany and her parents.

Then she got another surprise when Molly came into the room. Molly brought a handmade dress for Paige to wear to church. The stitches were so tiny. Molly hugged Karen, giving her a kiss on the cheek.

"Hi, sweetheart. How are you feeling? I can't wait to see and hold that baby girl of yours."

"We'll go up to the nursery, and we can both look at her."

Karen put on a bathrobe and house slippers. They walked slowly with Karen's arm around Molly's waist. They stopped in front of a sleeping baby.

The name tag read, "Paige E, Spanek, 21 inches, 7 pounds, 8 ounces." Her hair had a faint showing of blond.

"Isn't she the most precious thing you ever saw, Karen?"

"Sure, but then I am the proud mama, Molly."

They walked back to the room, visiting as they strolled along. Molly stayed only a short time and hesitated to mention how terrible things were next door.

That same afternoon, Reverend Wilcox called. He held Karen's hand. Her eyes glistened with tears as he prayed for her and Paige. Before leaving, he asked Karen to come to church as soon as she was able.

That evening, the Prathers visited Karen. They made over Paige, taking turns holding her. The following morning, Karen went home, driven by Tiffany. This new family member was certainly going to change Karen's life from now on.

CHAPTER 13

Upon arriving in the apartment, Karen laid Paige in the new baby bed Tiffany had purchased. Karen began the routine of making formula and folding clothes for Paige.

Karen placed a call to the County Service Center. The lady told her she would be eligible for day care assistance while she worked.

Two months had passed for the new mother and baby. Karen would take Paige for a stroll in a nearby park most evenings. One evening, she was sitting on a bench, enjoying the day when she noticed an older man sitting on a nearby bench.

His clothing was in a threadbare condition. *Perhaps he had fallen on hard times,* Karen thought. Oftentimes, he would be there when Karen and Paige arrived. He always came over to see Paige.

Karen could tell he appeared to be hungry. The following evening, she brought a sandwich for him. He told her his name was Walter Riebert. No other information was forthcoming at that time.

About a month later, Walter and Karen were visiting in the park, and he asked her where her husband was.

"Oh, Walter, you are a friend. I'll tell you everything."

She began with the trouble she had with her stepfather. Then she told him about with her date with Matt Dresser last fall. Karen related how she was raped by using rohypnol—a date rape drug.

She explained how he had dragged her out of his car and was left her in the park late at night. Karen told him how she was unconscious at the time from the drug. Also, that the police put her in jail and charged her with taking drugs.

"I found out I was pregnant and made the decision to keep my baby."

"Karen, you have had a terrible time, but I'm so proud of how you handled everything." Then Walter became very quiet, not speaking for a few moments. His face became pale as he tried to speak.

"Walter, are you all right? Can I take you to a doctor or somewhere?"

"Karen, I can help you in your case with Matt Dresser."

"No, Walter, there wasn't enough evidence or witnesses to convict him."

"Yes, there is, Karen."

"What do you mean, Walter? I don't understand."

Walter sat on the bench with her and began to explain. He told her about living in the park and being charged with vagrancy. He told her he was a witness when Matt Dresser dropped her in the park that night. Walter said he didn't come forward for fear of being charged with vagrancy again.

"Walter, will you help me now?"

"I sure will. Let's go to the police station right now."

They walked over to Karen's car at the curb. She put Paige in her car seat and unlocked the door for Walter to get in. Karen drove directly to the Stanton policy station, parking in front.

This time, it would be different going into the station, she thought.

She got Paige out of her car seat. Walter waited for her on the sidewalk. He held the door open for her to enter the station.

Sergeant Schultz was on duty at the desk. He looked hard at the two people approaching. A plainly dressed young woman with a little baby and an older man. The man seemed familiar somehow. He asked her how me might help her.

"I was involved in a rape case last fall. My name is Karen S. Spanek."

"I remember that case, ma'am, there was insufficient evidence."

"I have an eye witness who will come forward now."

Sergeant Schultz went into the detective offices then returned. An older man came forward, asking her and Walter to come in. He got seats for both of them.

He then went over to a large file cabinet and pulled out a large, bulging file. He scanned the material before speaking.

"Sergeant Schultz said you have some new evidence or a witness?"

Walter explained that he was in the park on the night Matt Dresser left Karen in the park. Then he related why he didn't come forth at that time.

"Would you sign a statement after I take it all down?"

"Yes, I would. Karen has suffered with this too long."

The detective took down Walter's entire story. Then he typed the statement on the proper forms. Walter then signed the forms spread out in front of him. He signed "Walter P. Riebert."

Karen felt a sense of vindication as she watched Walter sign the statement.

"Ms. Spanek, the department will contact you very soon. First, the district attorney will have to file to reopen the case. Mr. Riebert, with your testimony, justice will be done for this young lady."

Karen thanked him, and they left the station. Paige was beginning to get fussy. She would need to be fed soon. Karen realized the lateness of the hour, knowing both of them would need to eat.

"Walter, let's get something for our evening meal. I'm so grateful for your help in this. I'll stop for some hamburgers on the way home. We'll eat at my place, and then I'll take you home."

Walter was rather nervous. No one had dared to ask him into their home before. Karen could see that he was upset. She stopped for hamburgers and fries on the way home.

She drove to her apartment and parked her car. She carried Paige in, while Walter carried the food.

"It's all right, Walter. Only Paige and I live here."

Walter could see that she lived rather simply. *Where is my family now? Where are my two sisters living?* he wondered. Karen fed Paige and then put her down in her crib. She made coffee for Walter while he waited patiently at the table. He watched as Karen repeated a mealtime prayer.

They finished their food. *This is heaven,* he thought. He missed the scene of home and hearth.

"Walter, I can take you home now."

"No, it has been such a special day. I'm going to walk home. There is still daylight left anyway."

He arose to leave, and Karen gave him a hug. Tears came into his eyes at this gesture.

"I have no father, Walter. You've been like one to me.

I'm somehow going to repay and help you. Now people will believe me because of your bravery."

The case was to begin in August. All the people involved in the case were notified and subpoenaed. Karen was excused from work for the trial. It was held in downtown Capitol City. The public had been following the case in the daily newspaper.

In a more affluent part of Capitol City, a different scene was taking place. Matt Dresser was in a more sober train of thought as he faced his mother.

Clarissa Dresser was livid as she faced her son. She had finished talking with her lawyer and the private detective. They said that Matt's case didn't look good.

The lawyer she hired suggested Matt would most surely do time, if the DA had a witness. His sources didn't know of any witnesses.

* * *

Walter was now living in public housing. He was also working part-time. He would visit with Karen and Paige often. His life was better than ever now.

The case began on a Monday with Karen sitting at the DA's table. Matt sat with his lawyer. Both attorneys gave their opening statements. Matt's attorney asked that the case be dismissed due to lack of any new evidence. The judge refused his motion.

It was nearing the end of the trial when Walter was asked to testify. He told his story as he knew it. Matt's lawyer couldn't shake his story. Summations were made, and it was left to the jury.

Two hours later, the jury returned. The verdict read, "Guilty." Clarissa broke down in tears. The DA congratulated Karen.

She felt downcast. *What have I really won here today?* she thought.

Clarissa conferred with Matt's lawyer. Matt's attorney drew Karen aside for a moment. He told her that Clarissa Dresser wanted to see her. She was asking forgiveness for what her son had done. Karen was given an envelope containing a message.

The note read, "Please forgive this short note. How can any grandmother not love this little child? It will possibly be the only grandchild I shall ever have. I shall set up a trust for college when she is eighteen."

Karen first read the note, then looked over at Clarissa. She had to sit down for a few moments. Then she arose. Going over to Clarissa, she took her by the hand and said, "I'm sorry."

The trial was over, she and Walter walked to the car. Karen's thoughts were on just how she could help Walter find his family. She felt it was the Christian thing to do. He had helped prove her true character in the trial that had taken place.

She could recall Walter mentioning they lived in Ohio. Perhaps Detective Ray Crawford of the Stanton Police Department could help find Walter's family.

The next day, she went to see him personally. She was escorted into his office.

"Karen, what can I help you with today? This call is surely not about your case."

"No, Detective Crawford, I'm trying to locate Walter Riebert's family."

Karen filled him in on all she knew of Walter's family, especially his two sisters. She continued by telling him the children were born in Ohio. He listened, taking down the data.

"Let me work on this, Karen, and I'll get back to you."

* * *

On a quiet street in Warrensburg, Pennsylvania, the phone rang. It was answered by one of the two sisters living there. Previous failed marriages have drawn the sisters, Ruby and Fay, together.

"Ruby, that phone call was from some detective in another part of the state. It was from a city called Stanton. He also wanted to know if our maiden names were Riebert. He asked a funny question. 'Where were we born?' Very odd indeed."

"Fay, you can never tell who will be on the phone these days."

Three weeks later, Karen received a phone call from Detective Crawford. He had good news for her. He had traced the sisters to Warrensburg, Pennsylvania. He gave her their address and phone number.

Just then, Tiffany came in to visit Karen. Karen told her about locating Walter's sisters. She asked Tiffany how best to handle this news.

Tiffany suggested she and Karen buy Walter an airplane ticket to go see his sisters. They should let them visit on the phone first.

Karen phoned Walter to come over for a visit. Walter held Paige, just as he usually did when visiting with them. He could see that Tiffany and Karen were both excited about something. Karen spoke to him.

"Walter, Tiffany and I have some wonderful news. How would you like to see your sisters again?"

"That would be so nice. Just to be with them again would be all I'd want for the rest of my life."

Tiffany said, "Well, Walter, we know where they are living. You'll get to talk to them right now."

Karen quickly dialed a long distance number. She heard a voice say, "Riebert's residence." Karen explained, "Walter, your brother, is here and wants to talk with both you, ladies."

She could hear shouting and weeping in the background. Ruby was so excited and weeping she could barely speak.

"Oh, Walter, is that really you? We love you."

"Yes, it's really me. I thought of you two girls every day it seems."

The brother and two sisters filled a twenty-five-year gap in minutes. Each of them took turns crying and talking. Finally, Walter handed the phone to Karen. She explained everything to the sisters. Throughout this time, Karen could hear them say, "Bless you."

"Fay, you and Ruby be at the airport to pick him up tomorrow evening. He will be coming home then."

Tiffany and Karen took an excited Walter to the airport the next day. They walked with him to the ticket counter. He just kept hugging them and thanking them. They waved a final time as he boarded the plane.

On the way home, Tiffany said, "You would think that this only happens in Hollywood. But it happened right here in Capitol City."

She had only a short time before she would register for her fall classes in Capitol City University. She would be studying on her major courses from on. Karen established a routine with Paige. Her baby was easy to care for. After getting Paige ready for the day at the day care center, she would get ready for another day at KJCH.

The ads being developed would reflect on the coming months, which kept everyone busy. When fall classes started, she would have to only work part-time. The schedule of classes and work at the television station became a heavy burden for Karen.

It was early in the fall when she realized she would need a larger place to live. The small efficiency apartment worked well by herself, but with Paige and her crib in, it was just too small.

When evening came, Karen welcomed the night for rest as would have to get up in the night to feed Paige. Often, Tiffany would come over and visit on weekends. They would stroll Paige in a park near the apartment.

The two women agreed to take the next Monday off to enroll in Capitol City classes. Both knew just what courses they would need. Tiffany was now working for the state Department of Human Services.

The next Monday, they drove to the campus in Tiffany's car. They enjoyed the time away from work and the time together. Enrollment was easy from Karen as her scholarship papers had arrived from Grafton in Stanton.

The lady enrolling Karen remarked about her high grade average. "You won't have any trouble keeping your grades here with your background." Later, the two friends met, and Tiffany treated Karen to lunch.

Tiffany went with Karen to pick up Paige as hadn't seen her lately. Tiffany couldn't wait to hold Paige, who showed off for Tiffany. Finally, they went their separate ways.

When Karen arrived home, she fed Paige and laid her down for a nap. Karen went through her courses and leafed through her books. While she scanned the books, she knew that her goal of obtaining a degree was in sight.

The following Friday, she received a telephone call from Molly. Molly said she come over around lunch on Saturday and would also bring lunch for them.

"Now, Karen, don't scold Paige's grandmother. I must keep track of how our baby is doing."

The next morning, someone knocked on the door. She had two bags of groceries in her arms. Molly had bought some extra things for Karen. *What would I ever do without this beautiful woman standing before me,* Karen thought?

Molly enjoyed bathing Paige. It had been a long time since she had taken care of a little one. Molly finished dressing and feeding Paige, then rocked her to sleep.

Molly brought a quick and easy meal to prepare, and they were ready to enjoy a meal and each other's company. Molly asked Karen about Tiffany. When Paige awoke later, they both strolled her in the nearby park.

Molly didn't want to hurt Karen's by mentioning how dreadful the couple next door was behaving. She certainly couldn't understand how or what kept them together.

Early in the afternoon, Molly left to return home to Stanton. She didn't want to leave Karen alone. Thank heaven Karen was busy attending college classes and working.

Karen certainly wasn't at a loss for something to do. Fall classes began on campus. Karen was excellent at taking notes. When her classes were over, she would go to work at the station until five thirty or six in the evening.

She dreaded leaving Paige for so long at a time, but the day care workers adored their new charge.

CHAPTER 14

One evening, Karen looked through the usual junk mail. One letter was addressed from a large law firm in downtown Capitol City. *What could this be about?* she queried.

She placed the mail beside Paige as she set the baby's carrier down momentarily to unlock the door. Paige was obviously sleepy, so she fed her and laid her down in her crib.

Karen got a paring knife and carefully opened the letter. It was addressed to Karen S. Spanek. She read through the letter. It was about a fund being set aside for Paige Spanek's higher education. It was set up under the direction of one Clarissa Dresser. What Karen felt was not happiness about what had transpired in the last year, but now her child would be able to attend college more easily. Karen would take work home on weekends when she could.

She would study and sleep between bottles and feeding of this new little person who was hers alone now. *Somehow, I will persevere no matter what price I have to pay,* she would surmise.

The people in her area at work and the entire station respected her because of her determination. Her work was often outstanding helping the station make much-needed profit.

Karen applied for food stamps with help from Mrs. Adkins. She really hated to do this, but she was barely making it now with all her bills.

The stamps meant the difference between putting off eating to buy gas and paying rent. One Sunday, she drove to Stanton to go to church. Everyone greeted her with love and understanding. The women were all smiles as she brought Paige to be left in their care.

One Friday, as she went into the station to begin her afternoon work, Mr. Siegfried's secretary said, "Mr. Siegfried would like to see you a moment, Karen."

Karen had a worried look on her face as she was escorted into his office. He only smiled at her, asking her to take a seat for a moment.

"This is going to be a happy minute for you, Karen, not to worry. I'm going to give you a dollar raise, young lady. You have made a huge difference in our station since you have been here."

Karen got up and went around to give him a hug. She thanked him several times. He stood momentarily as he thought, *It's not often some really appreciates what is given them. This young lady is someone special.*

Karen's feet didn't like they were on the floor as she went to her desk. The day just flew for her that afternoon. God surely had a hand in her life as she said a quiet prayer at that moment.

The following Saturday, her church was having a shower for Paige. They treated her and Paige like queens. It was very enjoyable two hours. Everyone took turns holding Paige. There was clothing for Paige up through the age of two. The lunch was special and ended with a beautiful prayer for her and Paige. Her car was full as she drove back to Capitol City and her tiny apartment.

Tiffany came by in the afternoon to look at the clothing Paige received. Karen noticed one small package that she had missed before. Where had it come from?

Tiffany watched Karen take care to wrap the beautiful small package. She opened something wrapped in scented paper. Inside the paper laid a thick stack of money and a note from the women of the church signed by everyone present at the shower. Karen began to sob after reading it.

"What is the matter? What does the note say, Karen?"

> Dearest one, you have been going to this church since eight, and we love and care for you. You are not alone in your daily struggles. May God's face shine upon you and your little one this day.

Tiffany could only shake her head in amazement. Karen's church really cared for each other. That was evident. Tiffany could see God's hand in Karen's life Tiffany heard Paige awakening and went to pick her up. "My, how you are growing, sweetheart."

On Friday, Karen stopped to purchase a Capitol City newspaper at the local market. She would need an apartment there. *What a joy you are to me,* she mused while holding Paige.

Paige was beginning to smile and laugh now. Karen prepared a light meal, then bathed Paige, fed her, and put her down for the night.

Karen spread the classified ads on the kitchen table. She saw very little of Tiffany, who often worked late. Scanning the rental ads, she noticed a large garage apartment.

Karen circled it and two other ads. The next day, she and Paige would look at them. Karen awoke early to tend and feed Paige. She ate a quick bowl of cereal. After getting Paige ready, she placed her in the car seat. The time was 9:30 a.m.

She didn't want to wait until late in the day to go apartment hunting. Later, she was checking a Capitol City map. The first two apartments made her hesitate to rent them. They were in a rough part of town.

The third one was on Van Buren Street. She located that party of town. The homes were older, well-tended ones, rather stately. They were built in a different era and well landscaped.

Karen drove her '85 Pontiac slowly along Van Buren street. The homes there were built at least seventy years ago, she guessed.

Paige slept peacefully in her car seat. *I must find a larger place,* she thought. Coming into view was a large, white two-story home surrounded by a black handmade grill fence.

The house and grounds were immaculate. The flower gardens bloomed profusely with lovely roses. What love and care someone had given them. Karen drove into the driveway of a three-car garage. The ad had read simply, "Garage apartment." It was in her price range. There it was on the back of the garage with a walk leading to it.

She opened the car door after checking the sleeping baby. Standing at the gate, she looked toward the main house. An older man came out on the porch.

"Are you answering the ad, ma'am?" he asked.

He then approached Karen and opened the gate. Andrew Angus McLean, in his early seventies, extended his hand to her. She saw a six-foot, raw-boned, well-built man. His face had a quiet, almost haunted, look to it. He was neatly dressed in jeans and a blue work shirt and was clean-shaven. His sandy hair was sprinkled with streaks of gray. Karen felt the strong callused hand.

Glancing in the car, he saw a small sleeping child. His thoughts quickly turned to years ago and his beloved Ada. Ada's passing seven years ago still left him somewhat bitter and lonely. If only he and Ada could have had a family.

"Is it just you and the baby? No boyfriend or husband?" he inquired, looking into her blue eyes. He saw a young auburn haired woman in the early twenties.

There was a worried desperate look on her perfect complexioned face. She wore no makeup. The eyes were set in a Merle Oberon shaped face.

"No, only the baby and me." Karen answered. "No ex-husband or boyfriends," she added. "I'm finishing my junior and senior years at the university here. I have a small scholarship, plus I work part-time. Whatever it takes, I'm going to get an education. Mr. McLean, I'm a Christian, and I don't drink or run around."

Andrew had a slight burr to his speech. *Must be Scottish,* she surmised. Andrew liked the spunk five foot three young mother displayed.

"Well, let's go see the apartment." Then Andrew hesitated. "Will the wee one be all right?"

"I can't leave her for very long," she replied.

The furnished apartment was clean and very neat. They agreed on the rent, with Karen paying in advance. It would be exactly what she needed.

Karen started to walk back to the car, and Andrew said, "If you need to do any laundry, just come up to the house and knock. You can use my washer and dryer."

A big smile came over her face, "Bless you, Mr. McLean, thank you ever so much."

"This old house could stand more company," Andrew recollected as he watched Karen drive away.

Karen began the task of moving, after leaving Paige with Mrs. Henderson, her landlady. Mrs. Henderson said, "We will miss you and that little baby. This apartment is just too small for you and Paige."

The months that followed kept Karen busier than ever with work and classes. Andrew would only see her at night and on weekends. True to her word, no ex-husband or boyfriend came around. He enjoyed seeing her with the baby in the stroller.

There were only two occasional visitors. There was a tall, straw blond, outgoing girl and a stout, motherly woman driving an ancient car. Karen would always go to church on Sunday, he observed.

One Saturday morning, Andrew was approached by Karen. She was pushing a smiling blond-haired baby in a used baby carriage. Andrew was working in one of his flower beds.

"Good morning, Mr. McLean. How are you today? Mr. McLean, I bought a large beef roast. Would you share it with me tomorrow after church? I'm a good cook."

Andrew's face reddened slightly as he removed his gloves. He couldn't recall in ten years anyone giving him an invitation like this.

"I'll get home from church around twelve thirty, so come over then," Karen instructed.

"Why, thank you, Ms. Spanek. I'll be there." Andrew nodded.

Sunday was a beautiful day. Karen returned from church service. After changing and feeding Paige, she heard a knock on the door. Andrew stood there in new slacks and a matching shirt, wearing a pair of plain glasses.

"Come in," Karen said eagerly. The food smelled delicious. A pot roast was on the table, along with green beans, a small salad, hot rolls, and iced tea.

"The baby lay asleep on the bed in the next room. Please sit down, it's ready," she said. Karen bowed her head with Andrew joining her. She blessed all those there and the food, ending with a simple amen. He was drawn to her character and straight forwardness.

What parent wouldn't be proud of this wonderful young girl? he thought. The meal went pleasantly. Karen told him of her job at

Brown's restaurant since the age of sixteen. The meal over, he thanked Karen as he was about to leave.

"Let's call each other by our first names from now on, Karen," he requested.

Karen was touched by his humble thanks and suggestion. The next Saturday, she went to the main house to do some laundry. She paused at the door after knocking, calling, "Andrew, are you home?"

A voice answered, "Come in, Karen. I was in another part of the house."

"I need to use your washer and dryer please," she asked anxiously.

"Sure you can, help yourself."

He noticed Karen looked quiet, not like her usual bright and cheery self. The baby was in her stroller. Andrew helped lift the stroller up into the house. Karen noticed the house was neat and well kept. She immediately started a load of clothes.

The baby was busy with rattles and sucking on a pacifier. Andrew noted that Karen was a good and caring mother.

"I've just made a pot of coffee. Would you like a cup while you're waiting?" He poured two cups of coffee, placed them on an old-fashioned table, and sat down opposite Karen. He noticed that she was about to lose her composure.

She looked down at her hands, sipping her coffee. He lips began to tremble. Then she began to cry, needing someone to talk to.

"Oh, Andrew, I don't know what I'm going to do. My car won't start. I won't be able to get to work or school without a car. What will I do?" she sobbed. He handed her a large, clean blue workman's handkerchief

She slowly told him everything from the beginning. How her stepfather tried to molest her and moving out by herself. Then how her own mother refused to believe her story. She related how she worked on weekends to make ends meet while attending junior college.

She explained while working one weekend, she accepted a date with Matt Dresser. Then she told him about being drugged and how Matt Dresser put the drug in her tea. She related how he took her out in the country and raped her. She told Andrew how Matt dragged her out of his car and left her in the park at Stanton.

Sobbing, she continued telling how the police found her unconscious in the park afterward. How the police charged her with taking dope. About finding out that she was pregnant and refusing to have an abortion and keeping the baby.

"It's so hard being alone, Andrew. Sometimes, I don't know how I'll make it," Karen said, drying her eyes.

Andrew got up from his chair, went to her, and hugged her to him. Then Andrew began telling his story of being lonely since his beloved Ada died. His only nephew refused to visit him.

"You've been carrying a big load for such a wee one," he said, patting her. "From now on, you won't be alone, child, as long as I live," Andrew said, slightly sniffing. "Now about that old car of yours, you can drive Bessie. Bessie is like new, a seventy-five Buick, in the garage."

She tried to smile, hugging him with tears in her eyes. "Bless you, Andrew, and all the angels aren't in heaven. You are a Matthew 25:40, Andrew." He knew the Bible passage well. He gave her a set of keys.

"Monday morning, I'll have my garage work on your car and get it repaired. I don't want you worrying yourself and the little one. Dry your eyes now, child, just love that little blond baby there in the stroller." *What a tremendous responsibility it is to be all alone with no one to help or care for her,* Andrew thought. *What's life without helping or giving help to someone truly in need?* he philosophized.

The washing machine finished its last cycle. Karen put in another load and held the baby. Andrew asked to hold Paige for a while.

What a wonderful man he is, she mused. She left with the laundry, and Paige was pushed in the stroller by Andrew. They went to her apartment.

Moments later, she raised the garage door. There was a large, four-door, light blue Buick. It was just like new. Hesitating, she opened the door, then adjusted the seat. Using the keys Andrew had given her, she started the motor.

It started smoothly. Karen looked at all the different instruments on the panel in front of her. She carefully looked over the shifting lever, then slowly backed the car out of the garage. Looking over at the other bays, she noticed an older model pickup parked there.

Driving toward the grocery store, she noticed Paige nodding in her car seat. An hour later, she returned with sacks of groceries. After storing the groceries, she knocked on the kitchen door of the big house. Andrew came to the door.

"How did Bessie drive?" he asked.

"Just like a dream" she answered. "Andrew, I'm serving chicken fried steaks after church tomorrow, same time as before," Karen said, smiling up at him.

The next day, the older man and the young girl shared a simple meal together. Whey they had finished, Karen paused then said, "You know, Andrew, it's easier cooking for two than for one. Could I do the cooking for us and some of the housekeeping?" So the two shared life with one another.

Slowly, Karen began doing more of the housework and cooking for Andrew. She learned what his tastes and favorite dishes were. The two-story house was beautifully built. The rooms were spacious with wood flooring and wood-stained trim. Karen developed a systematic method of caring for it.

Andrew admired Karen more and more. She was a clean, caring, and a neat mother, always busy. Paige was a happy growing little baby.

One Saturday morning, there was a knock at the front door. *Just another salesperson,* Andrew thought. It was a rather tall young lady, about Karen's age. The young lady at the door was a strawberry blonde with a dazzling smile. She carried only her purse, no salespersons kit.

CHAPTER 15

Andrew opened the door, asking, "May I help you, ma'am?"

"Is Karen Spanek here? You must be Mr. Andrew McLain." Tiffany held out her hand to him. They shook hands. "I'm Tiffany Prather."

"Come in, come in, our Ms. Karen is upstairs. I'll call her. She will be so pleased that you have come to visit."

Karen smiled at both of them as she bounded down the stairs. Andrew could see the friendship the girls had for one another. They went into the kitchen with Karen pouring coffee for them. Karen then left, going into a bedroom to check on Paige. Tiffany followed her into the bedroom to see the sleeping child.

"You know that aunts are supposed to hold their nieces ever so often, Karen. Andrew, isn't that about the cutest baby you've ever seen?" Tiffany asked.

Andrew knew Karen had few friends, but the ones she had were neat people. They talked about work, fall classes, and Paige, of course.

"Andrew, Tiffany and I are meeting Molly to look for Paige some winter clothing. Would you mind cooking hamburgers on your grill later this afternoon?"

The girls left with Paige in her car seat. They spent about two hours with Molly, buying fall clothes. They returned in the afternoon with all the supplies.

They were going to have grilled hamburgers, potato salad, and baked beans. Andrew fired up his grill, a large expensive one—ready for charcoaling. He started grilling burgers and took note of Molly who cared for Karen and Tiffany. She treated Karen as any mother might.

Andrew had a table with a checkered tablecloth on it. They sat down together, enjoying the informal meal and each other. Evening was beginning to fall. All of them pitched in to clean everything up.

Andrew carried Paige's highchair back into the house. Paige had fallen asleep earlier. Finally, Molly and Tiffany left. Karen was sad to see them leave, saying, "You hate to see good friends leave."

The following Monday, Karen went to Capitol City University to enroll in her fall classes. Andrew watched Paige while she was away. Her job at KJCH was moving along nicely.

The weather began to change into winter. The clothes she had bought were a timely purchase for the cold, especially Paige's. The holiday season was near, and Karen decided against going to Tiffany's for any holidays. She and Andrew would have Thanksgiving and Christmas at Andrew's house.

Andrew bought an artificial tree for them to trim. He had boxes of lovely old-fashioned ornaments that were so pretty. They put up the decorations together.

Andrew really enjoyed this time together as he saw so little of Karen with her classes and work at the television station. Thanksgiving was near, and Karen purchased a small turkey to bake. She had the menu planned. Andrew was delighted that they would share the holidays together. One was a lonely number.

Thanksgiving arrived, and Karen had the turkey baking slowly in Andrew's gas oven. She had all the dinner finished by early afternoon. Andrew got out Ada's napkins, tablecloth, and flatware.

The table was set for three as Molly was coming for dinner. Molly arrived, bringing two pumpkin pies for dessert. She couldn't wait to hold Paige.

The baby was on her best behavior, smiling and generally showing off. The meal was ready. Andrew dressed for the occasion. Molly and Karen placed all the food on the table. The turkey was ready for him to carve. There were mashed potatoes, green beans, a special salad, hot rolls, and iced tea to go with it. There would be pumpkin pie for dessert.

They gathered at the table, sitting down with Paige in her high chair near Karen. They asked Andrew to say grace. Andrew became solemn, saying a beautiful prayer, with God, friendship, and peace in it.

"Where did one so young learn so much about cooking and housekeeping?" Andrew questioned.

Perhaps he was unaware she was around the kitchen cooks at Brown's. They treated her as their best friend. Also, her mother was a natural cook. They did justice to all the food. Molly left before evening, not wishing to drive after dark.

Karen's car ran like a dream after Andrew had it repaired. He never mentioned the cost to her. Gifts soon appeared under the Christmas tree. Karen left a picture of herself and Paige under the tree for Andrew. Andrew bought a gift certificate for a complete dress suit ensemble, and a fifty-dollar bill was also in the envelope. She also bought Andrew a fancy bird feeder.

Christmas morning, they opened their presents. She thanked Andrew by giving him a big hug. She could use the suit as her old one was quite worn. He loved the beautifully framed picture of a smiling Karen holding Paige on her lap.

For their Christmas meal, Karen baked a hen, with stuffing, vegetables, salad, hot rolls, and iced tea. Their meal was eaten late in the afternoon. Tiffany arrived then about the same time as Molly. All four exchanged more presents.

They visited and shared a cake that Tiffany had brought. Karen made coffee for them. The following months appeared to fly by. Spring was in full sway in Capitol City. Trees were leafing out. One more month and classes would end for Karen.

The days were warmer now, and Karen would often take Paige for a stroll in a nearby park. The flowerbeds were in full bloom. Work at the station was hectic but satisfying. Karen did more than her share.

Scott Chapin, her boss, appreciated her dedication and hard work. They both had children, but neither talked about their spouses. Both were conscious of this. She would drive away in an old Pontiac with a child seat in it.

Scott Chapin was a quiet man, never talking family with her. Karen noted a picture of a smiling little boy on his desk. He noticed she had a picture of a little baby girl on her desk.

One Friday, Scott and Karen walked to their cars at the same time. They exchanged small talk about the weekend. Then they drove away.

She is a very intelligent and very pretty, though plainly dressed, he thought. *She is driven to some goal. What is it?*

Scott glanced at the clock. It was almost time to be leaving, time to pick up Tyler at the nursery. His attention to this little four-year-old was delayed by someone's question.

"Scott, will we need to stay late for this project?" Karen asked.

Scott was project manager at KJCH television station. Karen was inquiring about the work they were both engrossed in. She was his best worker there but always very quiet about her personal life.

"No, this can be finished first thing Monday morning, Karen."

They left at the same time and walked to the parking lot together. When she opened the door of the old Pontiac, he again noticed a child's seat in the back.

Scott's thoughts turned to his own situation. Elaine, his wife of six years, had disappeared. He had no warning of this. Elaine had spoken occasionally about her misgivings of their son and marriage. It was still bewildering after she had been gone six months.

Scott had arrived home one evening in January to find she had departed. She left only a short note propped up on the napkin holder on the kitchen table. Most of her clothing and two hundred dollars from their checking account was all she had taken.

For some time afterward, Scott blamed himself for her actions. He talked first to Amanda Johnson, who worked with Elaine in an advertising company.

Amanda stated, "About all I know, she would leave for lunch and come back alone."

Elaine's boss added only one clue. Another of his employees had quit at the same time. But for Scott, life had to go on as he had his son Tyler. It was sad when Tyler from time to time would say, "Mama gone."

Scott could only hug him and say, "Mama gone." Work, church, and a few friends made life bearable these last months.

Scott heard a familiar voice on the phone ask for Elaine. "May I speak to Elaine a moment?" she asked hesitantly. "Gloria, Elaine isn't here. She left two weeks ago," he replied.

"What do you mean she left two weeks ago?" Gloria asked quietly. It was difficult explaining to Mrs. Marshall, his mother-in-law, on the phone.

"I came home with Tyler one evening, and all she left was a note on the kitchen table," Scott said. "She left without giving any idea where she was going or who she was going away with," he continued.

He didn't mention the conversation he had with Elaine's boss. Gloria Marshall hung up after telling him she would call back later. She hadn't come to see him or Tyler after that.

His mother offered all manner of support after this turn of events. His parents visited often, helping in so many ways. They cared for Tyler while Scott went to a business meeting in Los Angeles in the spring.

When he returned from his trip, he went to the law firm of Roland & Roland. He wanted legal advice about keeping Tyler. Elaine had abandoned the family and therefore had no legal right to Tyler.

In any event, he didn't want her to return and merely take Tyler. The law firm filed papers on Scott's behalf. They assured Scott of his legal rights. This action set his mind at ease.

Later, Mrs. Marshall called asking to baby sit Tyler, but Scott refused. Somehow, he knew that she knew where Elaine was living. Perhaps if he gave in, he might lose Tyler forever.

Then he recalled how he and Elaine had met. It was at a small southeastern college. Scott was a running back on the football team. This was his senior year. His plans were to work in communications, his chosen field.

The football scholarship helped him attain his goal. His team had won the game on the previous Saturday. It was a bruising four quarters of play. First, he would shower, then go to the dormitory to rest for a while. He would study for a couple of hours and then eat at the school cafeteria.

His appetite was such that he could eat anything. He came from a middle-class family, where food was sometimes a luxury. Perhaps later, he would go over to Charlie's to see who was there.

Charlie's place was noisy and full of the college crowd. Scott was greeted by several people after her arrived there. He heard, "Fine running, Scott."

One girl in a group near the jukebox smiled at Scott. She stuck her hand out at Scott, saying, "Hi, I'm Elaine Marshall."

Scott looked her over, noticing she was filled out in all the right places. He liked her expensive perfume. He asked her to dance, learning she was a senior art student. They made small talk while dancing.

Elaine wouldn't let go of him. They danced all evening. She finally said, "Let's go outside for some air. It's stuffy in here. My car is out front, come on." They got in a late model sport car. She asked him about his future plans.

He explained how his scholarship worked to help him in his education. They drove around, then parked in a quiet dark area of the college.

Scott carefully pulled her to him, kissing her. She then straddled his legs, kissing him long and hard. She sat back under the wheel. They kissed once more. She dropped him off at his dormitory around midnight.

Elaine kissed him once more, saying, "I'll call you real soon."

They met often between classes and after football practice. She suggested Scott meet her mother on a weekend after football season. He called his parents to tell them he would be away during Thanksgiving. It was only a seventy-mile ride to her house. The house was a lovely two-story, in an old well-kept neighborhood. Her mother had several guests there for the holiday. All of them asked Scott about his future plans.

Her mother and her guests left for a country club early in the evening. Scott and Elaine stayed home and watched a movie on television and ate popcorn.

Elaine turned the lights off. They kissed passionately while *lying* on the couch. Turning off the television, she said, "Let's go upstairs, Scott." She led him upstairs while holding his hand.

They went into a bedroom where she pulled him down on the bed. Then Elaine began to unbutton his shirt. Scott unbuttoned her blouse. They finished undressing, then pulled the covers down on the bed.

After much touching and feeling, they made love. It was getting quite late when Scott began to pick up his clothes before going to his room.

Later, Elaine's mother and her friends returned home. The house now became silent. Scott was awakened by a kiss; it was Elaine. She got in bed with him, unclothed.

"You'll get us in trouble, Elaine. What are you doing?"

"Mother sleeps like the dead. Let's make love again."

They made love again. Afterward, they lay in each other's arms, spent.

"Scott, you're great. But now, I must return to my room."

The Thanksgiving Day dinner was a masterpiece. Scott had never seen a table set so fine. Elaine's uncle said grace. Everyone did justice to the fine meal. The guests watched a football game and played various games.

The weather kept everyone inside. On Sunday, Scott and Elaine attended church with her mother. Early in the afternoon, Scott and Elaine returned to college. She dropped him off at his dormitory.

"Let's get together this week," she called as she drove away.

Football season ended, and spring arrived quickly. Finals were near, and Scott was interviewed for a television position on campus. He and Elaine had been dating steadily. They both graduated in May.

Scott's parents attended the graduation ceremonies and sat with Elaine's mother. After the ceremonies, Scott was packing to leave when Elaine walked into his room.

"What's going to happen to us, Scott? Will I get to see you anymore?"

Scott took her into his arms and asked her to marry him. The wedding was planned for the month of June. They both were caught up in a whirlwind of activity. The wedding took place in Elaine's church, and she looked like a vision in her expensive gown.

They went to St. Croix for their honeymoon. The happy couple settled down in Capitol City. Scott worked at the television station. Elaine was hired by an advertising company, doing graphics. They appeared to have it all going their way.

Their life was busy but an uneventful one. They were now in their second year of marriage. One evening, Scott let himself into the apartment to find Elaine on the couch crying and distraught.

"What's the matter, honey? Did you get fired?"

"It's worse than anything like that. I'm pregnant, and I wish I were dead. I'm not into parenting, ever!"

Scott sat on the couch next to her. "You'll love this little baby as time goes by. I'm sure many new mothers felt the same way at first."

The following months, Elaine's attitude never changed. Her mother, Grace, appeared happy about becoming a grandmother. Scott's parents were ecstatic about becoming grandparents. Elaine's attitude bothered Scott.

A little baby boy was born later. He was seven pounds, eight ounces, and twenty-one inches long. He was a beautiful little boy with a smattering of dark hair. Scott was so proud to be holding his own son. They named him Tyler.

Scott took over all the parenting chores. Elaine was more than glad to let him do everything. After Tyler's birth, their marriage became strained, not warm as it once was. Tyler was a happy baby with an outgoing personality.

Elaine used any excuse for not handling him. Scott tried to make up for her lack of caring. Taking care of his son was a no-brainer. He would always be there for his little baby boy.

People would make over Tyler when they were out in public. Elaine went along with the outpouring of people toward them, for that moment only.

CHAPTER 16

She gradually began to be away evenings and weekends. Scott was always alone with Tyler. He knew their marriage for all intents and purposes was over. Scott had no idea how all this would play out.

It was on a weekend alone when Scott discovered she was with someone else. Tyler became quite ill. He took him to an emergency ward of the hospital. The doctor placed Tyler in the hospital overnight for observation.

Tyler recovered enough the next day to go back home. Scott was relieved. He tried to call Elaine, who was away for an advertising conference for her company. Not having any emergency number, he contacted her boss for a hotel name and number.

"We didn't have any business trips scheduled this weekend anywhere. Is there anything I can help you with?"

"No, I have gotten mixed up on what Elaine's instructions about where she was supposed to be."

When she returned that Sunday evening, he said nothing to her about the call to her agency.

"How was the conference this weekend, Elaine?"

"It was great. We had lots of meetings all weekend long. I'm sure glad it's over. I'd rather be home with you and our baby." Though she made this statement, she never once picked up Tyler to hold him.

Scott's work at the television station kept him very busy. On most weekends, he would visit his parents. His parents knew there was trouble in the marriage, but never entered in the problem.

Many evenings, he would take Tyler for strolls in the park. On these occasions, she would hang up the phone immediately after he came back into the apartment. It was someone other than one of her odd and unusual friends.

One such time, she began to sob, caught herself, and rubbed the tears from her eyes. At times, she would stare at Scott and the baby, never speaking.

Late spring came to Capitol City. The work day over, Scott once again went to pick up Tyler to begin another lonely evening. All the nursery workers were especially attached to Tyler. It was a Friday evening, and Scott was tired. He hoped on hope Elaine would have supper started.

He and Tyler bade the nursery workers good-bye and drove home. He turned at the end of the street. Elaine's car wasn't in its usual place. Where could she be at this hour?

He unbuckled Tyler from his car seat and carried him into the apartment. The apartment was completely silent. Not a light was turned on, only darkness and the ticking of a clock.

Scott took Tyler's outer clothes off and turned on some lights. Somehow, Scott knew Elaine wouldn't be returning to them. *Why wouldn't I know this, in view of her comings and goings?* he thought. He went into the kitchen and saw a note propped up on the table.

He read through the letter twice. Never had he felt so alone as he did at this moment. "Why? Wasn't marriage and child enough for her?"

Regardless of the past, Scott's thoughts were on his and Tyler's future. He would make the best of it. Scott concerned himself with the evening meal. He heated up food and fed Tyler. He was glad that Tyler was a good baby. Tyler didn't eat well, only tasting his food.

After bathing Tyler and putting him down for the night, Scott called his parents. The time was seven in the evening when he called. His mother answered the phone, "Chapins."

"It's me, Mom."

"How's that little sweetheart boy doing? Is there anything wrong, son?"

"That's what I am calling you about, Mom. When I got home this evening, there was a note on the kitchen table. She's gone."

He continued relating all that had transpired during the preceding months. Mable Chapin was from a different time and era. You stayed with your life partner. She asked him if she could be of any help.

He refused her offer of help. He could feel the effect this news had on his mother. She told him she was hurt to hear the news. A little boy was now without a mother.

Mable, like any other mother, felt obligated to help her one and only child. There was never any doubt about her feelings for her son and grandchild. Before hanging up, she said, "I'll pray for you and my little grandson. Also, I know that God will put someone in your life who will love you and Tyler."

He hung up the phone with tears in his eyes. He just sat for a while, thinking of what the future held for him and Tyler. One thing for sure, he would start going to church again next Sunday.

Scott decided to take an evening college class. The days began to warm up now. Very often, he would take Tyler for a stroll in the park nearby.

One such day on a Saturday, he and Tyler were in the park. It was a gorgeous day. He was resting on a bench, his thoughts turned to his staff at the television station. He wondered about one young woman who worked there by the name of Karen Spanek.

She was very intelligent and was easy to work with. But he knew little of her private life. Scott only knew that she had a little baby girl, a few months old. He was almost asleep when he heard the sound of a baby nearby. The reverie was broken by someone calling his name.

"Hi, Scott. I didn't know you had a little boy."

Turning, he saw Karen Spanek pushing a baby girl in a new stroller. "Hello, Karen, fancy meeting you here like this. Sit down and let's visit," he found himself saying.

Both were hesitant about starting any conversation. They both laughed about their work and the funny happenings around the station. They were sitting beside each other now. Scott looked deeply into Karen's face. She smiled back at him, a calm came over him. Something impelled him to confide in her. He became quiet.

"Scott, is everything all right?" she asked.

"My life has been completely torn apart since Friday evening."

Karen placed her hand on his. "Scott, there are many things I have wanted to tell you but couldn't until now. Oh, Scott, it's so difficult to tell what has happened to me this last year."

"You don't have to tell me, Karen, if you don't want to."

She began to tell him everything about her childhood, work, school, stepfather, and now living alone. Karen finished and was crying softly.

"Such a terrible load for you to carry alone," Scott averred.

"You are a very intelligent person and superb at your work at the station. We couldn't do it without you," he said, handing her his handkerchief. He then grew quiet, not knowing how to begin.

She could see tears forming in his eyes as he spoke. He talked of his parents, hopes, and dreams. How he went through college on a football scholarship. Then finished by telling her all about his wife, Elaine. How she was running around behind his back and never loving their little son. He told her about the letter he had found on the kitchen table last Friday.

"From now on, I'm going to be a better person for my little son. This Sunday, I'm going back to church."

They looked at each other at the same time. "You're a good man, Scott. Whatever could your wife be thinking? You at least have parents that care for you."

"Karen, if I can ever help, just let me know. Let's begin by doing things together."

"I would like that very much, Scott."

They both rose from the park bench, pushing their babies through the park. The park never looked so good to them than at that moment. The birds were singing, and the flowers in full bloom were everywhere.

They each had the feeling that everything would be all right from now on because they would be there for each other. Though unspoken, Scott and Karen felt they were together now and in the future. Each felt a tremendous load life off their shoulders. They went their separate ways. They exchanged addresses and telephone numbers before parting.

The summer months were busy ones for Karen. One Saturday, Karen planned a picnic. All the staff at the television station was invited, along with Scott, Tiffany, and Molly. It was a nice size group that attended. Picnic tables were set up by Andrew in the backyard near his barbecue.

Andrew was proud to be a part of all these young people. Tiffany and Scott got to meet each other. Scott liked the tall, brassy, strawberry blond. There was plenty of food. Croquet was set up, and everyone took part. They joked about one another's skill level.

There was much laughing after playing games of all kinds. Prizes were given out for every reason and excuse. Tiffany won the croquet competition. Molly was content just to hold both Paige and Tyler. She was happy in her role as grandmother.

Everyone ate and retired to blankets spread in Andrew's backyard. Andrew was delighted to have them enjoy his beautifully kept yard. They were under large shade trees.

Finally, by late afternoon, everyone drifted off to their own homes. The women gave Andrew hugs as they departed.

He told them, "Please come back and see me soon."

"Andrew, I must put this baby down for a nap. May I help you put all this equipment away?"

"No, I'll do that later. I'm going to watch the evening news first. I don't know when I've had so much fun."

The next week, Andrew was alone at the home. Karen was attending college and would be home after work. *She had such a tremendous daily load it would kill anyone else,* he thought. But Karen seemed to go on, always upbeat.

The Christian person was shown through her work and her friends about her. Andrew enjoyed having Karen and her baby live with him. They were both such wonderful company. There were also her many friends she had introduced him to. A smile lit up his face as he recalled he picnic.

He hadn't been feeling well as of late. What would become of his house, its grounds, and his estate? Andrew's thoughts were on these things as Karen drove up. She greeted him with a smile.

He remembered Karen had no family, only close friends. She brought love and contentment to him. None of his relatives cared to call or visit him. Karen cooked and cleaned for him, never asking for anything in return. What would his life be without this beautiful outgoing young woman?

She would be the only one to bring anything like a granddaughter into his life. An idea began to form in his mind. What he was about to do would make his few relatives furious. Let them be mad. It was his life and estate to do with as he saw fit.

The next day after breakfast, he called his lawyer. He made an appointment that morning. He returned from the bedroom dressed to leave. A fireproof box was placed on the kitchen table. Andrew selected a few papers from it.

Locking the house, he went to the garage. The garage door opened automatically. He backed the older model Buick out. Then he drove downtown to his lawyer's office.

Getting off the elevator, he was quickly standing in front of a secretary's desk. The young secretary looked up at an older gentleman with gray hair standing before her.

"You must be Mr. Andrew McClain? Do you have an appointment, sir?"

"I want to change my will. I talked with someone earlier this morning."

Andrew was escorted into Mr. Blair's office, the senior member of the firm. Bill Blair rose and shook Andrew's hand. He asked Andrew to be seated. He looked over the papers carefully. They contained a list of all of Andrew's assets and property.

He had the secretary make the changes Andrew requested and handed the papers back to him. It was exactly what Andrew desired. Then Andrew wrote him a check for his fee. On the way home, he knew he had done the right thing.

He drove home carefully, with his beloved Ada on his mind. Soon he was parking Betsy in the garage. He could smell a meal being cooked as he neared the house. It smelled delicious.

Opening the door, he was greeted by Karen. Paige was playing on the floor. To him, these two were like his own.

"I went ahead and started supper, Andrew. It will be ready soon. Would you mind if I invited Scott and his little boy to share our meal?"

There was a knock on the door. Andrew answered it. There on the porch was Scott holding Tyler in his arms.

"Come in this house, you two, our cook has supper almost prepared."

"Hi, Andrew. Could you hold Tyler for just a moment?"

Scott took Tyler's coat off and put him on the floor to play with Paige. Andrew played with the children. He could see the attraction Scott and Karen had for each other. Scott thanked Karen for asking them over for supper.

Scott began to set the table. Two high chairs were set up next to the table for the little ones. Karen began bringing the food in from the kitchen. There was roast beef, mashed potatoes, vegetables, and a salad. Scott filled glasses with ice and tea.

They took their seats at the table. They held hands while Scott said grace quietly. The two babies ate but made a mess of their plates. The house quiet was broken by everyone making small talk, which Andrew enjoyed. He loved the harmony of these moments.

Scott and Karen cleaned up the kitchen together. Meanwhile, Andrew watched the little ones in the living room. Scott and Karen talked excitedly with each other. Andrew knew there was more than friendship between them.

The time flew by, and now it was only two months away from senior year for Tiffany and Karen. One evening, Tiffany knocked on the front door. She was greeted by Andrew.

"Get in this house, young lady."

"Give me a hug, Mr. McClain," Tiffany said.

"Now, Tiffany, you know my name is Andrew!"

Karen was in the kitchen working when Tiffany came in the house. Tiffany saw Paige walking around the coffee table. Andrew glowed when she swept Paige up in her arms.

"Come here to Aunt Tiffany, young'un." She and Andrew laughed together, enjoying each other's company.

Karen came into the room to join them. The two young women made a small talk about graduation.

"What are you going to do after graduation?" Tiffany asked.

"I'm staying here with Andrew, if he'll put up with Paige and me."

Graduation was just two weeks away for Karen. Scott and Karen had been dating for almost a year. They had done many things together—movies, church, spending time together at Andrew's house. Andrew told them they might as well get married because they were together so often.

On Saturday, they went to the park with the babies. Karen noticed Scott was unusually quiet. She knew long ago that she was in love with him. They were sitting on a park bench, watching their children when Scott took her by the hand. He looked into her eyes, asking her, "Would you marry me?"

"Yes, I will. My life would be so blue without you." They held each other and kissed.

"I'd better make it official," Scott said.

He pulled a small velvet box from his pocket. Then he placed an engagement ring on her finger. It was a large marquise cut diamond mounted on a gold band. She held out her hand in the sunlight and watched the diamond sparkle.

"Oh, Scott, I'll be a good wife to you." Tears were in her eyes as she hugged him again.

"I know we were meant for each other," he exclaimed. "One thing about it, we'll have a ready-made family." They both laughed. "We must go visit my parents." They planned to go the following weekend.

The next week passed quickly for Scott. Thursday evening, he had just arrived home with Tyler when there was a knock on the door. Tyler walked behind him as he went to answer the door.

CHAPTER 17

There stood Elaine. She tried to smile as if nothing had ever happened. She attempted to take Scott in her arms, but he held her away from him. She looked ten years older, a cigarette hung from her mouth. Elaine smiled at him as though she had just gone out for a Pepsi.

"Scott, may I come in?"

"Sure, but don't plan on staying."

Elaine looked down at Tyler clinging to Scott's leg. "Is this my little man? Come here to Mama." She tried to take Tyler in her arms, but he held on to his father's leg. Then he began to cry. "Come on, let me hold you, sweetheart."

"He doesn't want you to hold him, Elaine."

Scott could smell the heavy odor of liquor on her clothes and breath. Elaine became irate. Then she started screaming at him. Scott took Tyler in his arms, comforting him.

"You aren't taking him anywhere. I've gone through the courts since you left us, Elaine. If you don't leave, I'll call the police." He picked up the telephone, preparing to dial it.

She stubbed her cigarette out on the polished floor. Her face turned an angry red. "You haven't seen the last of me, Scott, I'll get a lawyer."

"Don't ever come here again, Elaine," he said.

She marched out of the apartment, slamming the door. He could hear the car tires screeching as she drove away. He soothed Tyler. Tyler quit crying and began to play with his toys on the floor. Scott called Karen, telling her about Elaine showing up at his door. They chatted for a while, discussing their trip to his parents. After hanging up, Scott telephoned his parents and told them he would be visiting them on the weekend. He told them that he and Karen had become engaged, and that she was eager to meet them. They were eager to meet her also.

Friday evening, Scott went over to Andrew's house to pick up Karen and Paige. It was only a three-hour drive. Paige and Tyler were on their best behavior during the trip. They stopped to eat on the way.

The city of Lansing was a small one. It was clean and neat, showing much pride of the residents. The sign read, "Lansing population, twelve thousand."

Scott drove in the driveway of an immaculate ranch-style house. It looked just like a postcard house. Scott looked over at Karen. She was nearly in tears and was quite nervous.

"My parents are going to love you, honey. They think you're a saint."

The front door opened and a smiling, older couple came out to the car. Margaret Chapin went to Karen, hugging her. So did John Chapin.

They helped take Paige and Tyler out of their car seats. John held Tyler, while Margaret held Paige. Paige smiled and wrinkled her nose, riding in Margaret's arms. Scott and Karen held hands as they walked into the house. Paige took to "Grandmother Margaret," and Margaret was taken with the blond, blue-eyed two-year-old.

They went into the kitchen to give the little ones a drink. Karen recognized the love that was in Scott's parents. She immediately felt at ease around them. Margaret asked her about Andrew's health.

"Andrew hasn't been well lately," Karen answered. "He went to the doctor last week, and they are going to run some more tests next week."

"Scott tells me you're a very good cook and housekeeper."

"Well, I've been cooking for both of us. It's easier for two, rather than one. I've been cooking since I was ten or twelve. My mother is an excellent cook. But I haven't seen her in quite some time."

Margaret drew Karen to her. "You poor dear. I'm so sorry."

The house was well kept, clean as a pin.

"Heaven's sake, let's go into the living room," Margaret said.

John and Scott made small talk. Both of his parents were taken with the children. John brought toys out for the two children. Paige kept bringing her toys over to Scott's mother. They got along famously.

It was early evening and nearing bedtime for the children. Scott bathed Tyler, and Karen bathed Paige. The children were brought back into the living room. Paige wanted Margaret to rock her. This thrilled Margaret.

Finally, both children were put to bed. Karen, Scott, and his parents went out on the front porch to swing and chat. For Karen, it was so peaceful.

"Thank you for having me here this weekend. It's so peaceful here."

Margaret answered, "Come and visit us anytime, but be sure to bring Paige."

Scott and Karen were in the swing. Karen's head began to nod. She caught herself "I'm going to have to join Paige. I can't keep my eyes open."

She went over to hug Scott's parents, then went over to give Scott a kiss. She then went to bed.

The next morning was the beginning of a beautiful day. All the family gathered in the kitchen for breakfast. Margaret prepared a wonderful meal. It was nice to eat a meal just once that you didn't have to prepare, Karen thought.

Karen helped Margaret clean up the kitchen while Scott and his dad strolled with the children. "Oh, Margaret, this is so neat to have parents who love you. I've been alone for so long. I'm going to be the best wife I can be for Scott."

"I know you will, Karen. You've done so much alone," Margaret said.

"This is your home now, and we are going to be parents to you from now on."

They all attended church together, then returned home afterward to have lunch.

The weekend closed quickly. Scott and Karen began to load the car for their return to Capitol City. They got in the car, and Scott began to back out of the driveway. His parents stood outside, waving.

"Oh, wait, Scott—stop!"

He wondered what could be wrong. He stopped. Karen got out of the car and ran to Scott's parents, hugging them both tightly.

"Thanks again for having me. I love you both." There were tears in her eyes as she returned to the car. She waved to them as Scott drove away. "Scott, your parents are such beautiful people. You are so lucky."

"When we get married, we'll be lucky also," he answered.

Arriving back in Capitol City, they drove up to Andrew's house. Scott helped Karen unload her bags, and Karen unbuckled Paige from her seat. Andrew came outside to greet them.

"I've missed you two this weekend."

Karen hugged and kissed Scott before he drove away.

The apartment was quiet when Scott let himself in. He heated some food for Tyler's evening meal. Then someone knocked on the door. It was Sunday evening.

Who could be calling at this hour? The man was plainly dressed. It was a process server. He handed Scott a legal document.

He dressed Tyler for bed and put him in his crib. Scott sat down to read the document. Elaine had begun legal action to take Tyler from him.

Scott told Karen about Elaine's legal action. "She doesn't have a case, does she, Scott?" Scott called his lawyer, then he told Karen, "My lawyer said abandonment for four years is a long time."

Scott took Karen aside to talk with her. "When this court action is over, let's get married right away, Karen."

"I don't want to wait any longer either."

Two weeks later, Scott's case came up on the court docket. His lawyer had prepared a solid case. He informed Scott that Elaine didn't have a chance. The judge sitting on this case was always for the child's best interest.

Karen and Tiffany attended to give Scott moral support. Elaine's lawyer gave the first presentation, finishing by requesting that Tyler be given to Elaine. It was a nonjury trial. Scott's lawyer had several witnesses. They testified about Elaine's character and leaving Scott and Tyler.

They also testified about her living with another man and about her heavy drinking. On the witness stand, Elaine was questioned about her living with a married man and her drinking. Scott's lawyer gave the judge the note she had left on the kitchen table.

Finally, both lawyers had presented their cases, and the judge asked for a short recess. Scott and his lawyer remained at their table. Karen said a silent prayer for Scott.

The judge came back to the bench. "I have read and listened to all the details of this case and have come to a decision. I deny Elaine Chapin's request for custody of Tyler Chapin." He then pounded his gavel, saying, "This case is closed."

Scott couldn't speak for a moment. Then he shook his lawyer's hand. Karen and Tiffany went over to Scott, hugging him.

"Karen, it looks like wedding bells for us," Scott said quietly.

"What's that you said, Scott?" Tiffany asked.

"He asked me to marry him when this case is over."

"Well, congratulations, you two," Tiffany said, hugging them.

"Tiffany, you are to be the maid of honor."

"Where are you going to have the ceremony?"

They all walked out of the courthouse together. "I'm going to ask Andrew if we can have it at his house, in the backyard."

Scott kissed Karen, saying, "See you at Andrew's house."

Karen and Scott drove up at Andrew's at the same time.

They got Paige and Tyler out of their car seats. Both children went to play in a sandbox Andrew had made for them. Karen and Scott held hands as they went into the house. Andrew looked out the window at them and smiled.

This young couple and those babies were about all the family he would ever have, he mused. Karen opened the door, saying, "Andrew, are you home? We have a question to ask you."

He came out of a back bedroom, asking, "What have you two been doing today?"

They filled him in on the court case. They sat together on the sofa, holding hands. Andrew knew these two were meant for each other. Momentarily, everyone was very quiet. They looked at Andrew, hesitating.

Then Karen began to speak. "Andrew, you know Scott and I are engaged. This court case is now over, and we wish to get married. We have two questions to ask you. May we have our wedding in your lawn three weeks from now? And secondly, would you give me away as I have no dad except you, Andrew?"

"Yes, you may, and I am honored that you asked me."

"Our plan is to have about thirty guests. Our pastor will officiate."

"Scott, your parents can stay here overnight as we have plenty of room. This big old two-story has many rooms."

Andrew went over to them, hugging them both. His eyes moistened as he did so. No one cared for him as these two fine young people did.

"Well, we better get to planning. I must be sure to call Molly."

They went into the kitchen where Karen served them tea. Nearly two hours later, their wedding plans were almost finished. Guests, catering, seating, flowers, and everything were arranged.

The wedding guest list was complete. Karen would phone Tiffany, who was to be her maid of honor. Molly was the first guest listed. Wedding announcements were to be mailed Monday. Scott would have a friend from college as his best man.

Scott's parents were called. They were excited about the news. They made arrangements for their pastor to officiate. Karen asked Tiffany to help her choose a wedding gown the following week. They hired a professional photographer.

The time was to be the first Saturday in June at 2:00 p.m. All the wedding plans were complete now. Andrew insisted the young couple live at his house when they returned from their honeymoon.

They were busy the next three weeks, getting ready for the wedding. The weather was to be perfect for the occasion. Scott's parents came on Thursday before the wedding.

Scott's parents helped in every way they could. They were delighted that Tyler and Paige would be their grandchildren. They would babysit the children while Scott and Karen went on their honeymoon. Karen and Scott would be gone for a week. Andrew purchased airline tickets to New Orleans for them as a wedding present.

Tiffany helped Karen pack her trousseau. The days that followed were enjoyed by them all, especially Andrew. Friday night,

Karen could hardly sleep, thinking about the next day that would change her life forever.

Breakfast was to be a light meal. The caterers came early to set up the tables and chairs. A small stage was decked out with flowers and lattice for the couple's ceremony. It looked so elegant.

In another part of the lawn, a table was set up for the cake and refreshments. Karen watched them set up all the different items. She was surprised to see a dance floor being laid out on the lawn. Andrew stood with her, smiling.

"Every wedding should have music and dancing."

Karen went inside to dress for her wedding. She was helped by Scott's mother. Guests began to arrive. The food had been brought in, and the cake looked beautiful. The champagne bowl bubbled, filled to the brim. A four-piece band played softly.

After she finished dressing, Karen asked Andrew to come into her room. Her gown fit perfectly. He saw how lovely she looked standing there. The dark auburn hair, light cream skin, and blue eyes made a gorgeous picture. Her makeup was simple and lightly applied.

She took Andrew's hand and choked back the tears in her eyes. "Thank you, Andrew, for being so kind to Paige and me. You've been there for me when I had no one."

For a moment, Andrew could hardly answer. Not one of his relatives treated him as well as this young woman standing before him did.

"I was so lonely until you came here," he said, answering her.

Molly stepped into the room. "You look stunning, Karen." Molly straightened out the train of Karen's dress. She looked at both of them and smiled. "Isn't this just like a picture, Andrew? Ten minutes to go, sweetheart."

The guests were all seated under the huge trees. Everyone was talking and laughing. They were all well dressed. The head television executives and their wives were in attendance.

All of Karen and Scott's friends at the station were there. Andrew had just mowed the lawn, and the yard was at its very best. Flowers were blooming everywhere; birds were heard chirping and singing. The band began to play the wedding march.

Molly was seated in a chair near where Andrew would be sitting. The guests quieted down as the music played. Scott and his best man waited for Karen to walk down the aisle.

His best man was a friend who played football with him in college. Gary was well dressed in an expensive suit. The band continued to play as Karen began to walk slowly down the aisle, with Andrew walking beside her. Andrew was dressed in a new blue suit and looked dashing. All heads turned to watch her. Karen dropped her hand from Andrew's arm. Scott felt so proud as she stopped near him.

The band stopped playing, and the pastor asked, "Who gives this bride?"

"Molly and I do," Andrew stated.

Molly dabbed at the tears in her eyes as Andrew took his seat beside her. They were seated in the front row.

The pastor charged the couple before him with the rules for a good marriage. Then the rings were produced. He finished by saying, "You may kiss the bride. I now give you Mr. and Mrs. Scott Chapin."

After the vows were exchanged, Scott and Karen moved to the three-tiered cake. They cut the cake together. The photographer was busy taking shots of all the proceedings.

CHAPTER 18

"Come on, Molly and Andrew, get your picture taken with us." Scott's parents were included in the picture taking.

Tiffany was all smiles as she stood for a picture with them. "I thought you two would never tie the knot." She looked beautiful, wearing a blue dress. Her strawberry colored hair was shoulder-length.

Then Scott's television friends proposed a toast. Everyone raised their glasses. The caterers refilled the fountain with more champagne. The guests queued up to enjoy the feast set up on the serving tables. The guests congratulated the young couple, with Scott's parents, Molly, and Andrew standing in line with them.

Scott's parents brought the children outside. Paige and Tyler were dressed in their Sunday's best. Scott held Paige while Karen held Tyler. The two little ones smiled like veteran actors.

The band began to play again. The guests stood back to let Scott and Karen took the first turn around the floor. They looked elegant as they twirled and turned. They had been practicing.

All the eligible women were grouped up for the bouquet to be thrown. Tiffany caught the bouquet, and everyone cheered for her. Scott and Karen had an airline flight to catch for New Orleans.

They went inside to change and finish packing. Changed and packed, Scott's best man and Tiffany took the couple to the airport. Before they left, the guests threw rice on them for good luck.

"Scott and Karen, we will see that everything is cleaned up, so don't worry about a thing. Have a nice trip. You two deserve it."

After their flight had taken off, they were embarrassed by the captain's announcement. He told everyone of their wedding that afternoon.

"Please hold my hand, Scott," Karen said.

They arrived at the New Orleans airport early in the evening. The shuttle took them to an upscale hotel downtown. They walked to the desk, holding hands.

Scott checked on their reservations. Karen watched proudly as Scott signed the register, "Mr. and Mrs. Scott Chapin."

They were booked in the bridal suite. The hotel had much old world charm. The bellman showed them the amenities of the suite then left them. Scott gave him a handsome tip. They immediately went into each other's arms. Minutes later, they were in bed where they made passionate love.

Later, Scott asked, "Are you hungry, or do you want to go sight-seeing, honey?"

She lay in bed smiling, shaking her head no. "Come back to bed, Scott."

They both slept well that night. The next morning, they went downstairs for a leisurely breakfast. Breakfast over, they just walked around the city. The week went by quickly for the newly married couple. They took sightseeing tours of New Orleans and the old mansions there.

On Friday, they took a shuttle to the airport. By early after-noon, they were home. They took a taxi to Andrew's house to change before going to Scott's parents. They were eager to see Paige and Tyler. They stayed for a short time visiting with Margaret and John, the happy grandparents. Finally, they returned to Andrew's. They were home to stay.

The following week was a busy one for Scott and Karen. There were many new projects at the television station and old ones to finish up. Andrew was happy to see them and the children back at the house.

Karen noticed he didn't look well. Perhaps it was only a touch of the flu. Karen was happy the weekend was coming. The work at the station was heavy due to extra ads.

On Friday, when Scott and Karen arrived home with the children, they didn't see Andrew anywhere. Karen went into his bedroom. He appeared to be unconscious. Scott immediately called 911.

In moments, a Capitol City ambulance arrived at the house. The ambulance crew gave Andrew oxygen before transporting him to the hospital. Karen was beside him. She got into the ambulance to ride with Andrew. Minutes later, they drove up to the hospital emergency entrance. Karen went into the waiting room.

Her mind went back to the first time they met. This wise and wonderful old man had been her only loved one. It didn't look good for him. She called Scott to say there wasn't any news.

An hour later, a doctor Lindstrom came out to see her. He was Andrew's doctor. Karen introduced herself.

"I've heard Andrew speak of you and the baby. He is in very grave danger. His heart isn't very strong and has looked so much better since you have been there with him."

Karen began to weep. "He has been like a parent to me. Why do the ones who mean the most to us have to die?"

The doctor looked at the young woman weeping, and then he spoke. "We don't know God's timing in all this. I'll be more able to give you a time frame in the morning."

She telephoned Scott first, then Molly. Karen decided to stay overnight at Andrew's bedside. Early in the evening, Andrew regained consciousness. Someone was holding his hand. His eyes began to focus; it was Karen.

What love and loyalty this young person has, he thought. Her face was framed by the low light in the room. Her eyes were red from weeping.

"How is my little mother? Are the children with Scott? How are you holding up?"

"Oh, Andrew, don't leave me. You're the only parent I have. I've loved you as my own." A smile played on his face. "I'll have to find a place to live now, Andrew."

He spoke in halting phrases, "Little one, everything will be all right, you'll see. Look in my Bible."

Then he sank into a coma. Karen never left his side except to change clothes. This was his condition until Thursday.

Dr. Lindstrom talked with Karen outside the room, "Karen, you must be brave. He has only a few hours to live."

Around eleven o'clock, Karen was sitting alone with Andrew. She placed her hand on his brow, smoothing his gray hair. His eyes opened briefly, and then his chest rose one last time. Andrew McClaren was gone.

She walked from the room with her face in her hands. Strong arms held her close; it was her husband, Scott. Karen began to weep inconsolably.

"Scott, hold me and never let me go. We still have your folks, thank heaven. Sweetheart, let's go home."

The house was strangely quiet as they entered it. Margaret and John were keeping Tyler and Paige. Karen went straight to bed, sleeping soundly. She awoke feeling better. Then she wondered what she should do about the funeral planning.

Then she remembered Andrew's instructions. Going to the Bible, she saw a long envelope in the front of it. On the front of the envelope read, "To be opened upon my death."

Karen and Scott read the instructions together. The entire funeral had been preplanned. Karen called the funeral home name there. The funeral home director asked her help in only some small details. She and Scott called in an obituary to the Capitol City Times. They tried to call a nephew, but to no avail.

The phone rang frequently during the weekend. The people phoning were Andrew's closest friends. They thanked Karen for being there for Andrew. One caller explained, "Andrew often talked of you and how proud he was of you."

Monday was a beautiful day for Andrew's one o'clock service. At twelve thirty, a funeral limousine drove up to the house. An elderly gentleman was sitting in his car in front of the house. He was a friend of Andrews. Karen went to him, asking him to ride with them in the limousine.

Karen, Scott, Tiffany, and Molly rode with him in the limousine. A graveside service was held. Many of Andrew's friends attended. Karen introduced everyone. She hugged them all.

There were banks of flowers. It was a dignified service, and Andrew was laid to rest beside his beloved wife Ada. After the casket was closed, everyone was given a rose to place on it. Andrew's friends shook hands with each of them before leaving.

The next day, Scott and Karen went back to work. Karen was worried about where they would live. Andrew's letter only said they could stay in the house as long as they wished. Friday, Karen was called to the lobby of the station. A man introduced himself as a member of a local law firm.

"Mrs. Chapin, would you please show me your driver's license?" She thought this was an unusual request. "Do you have a private place where we could talk in private?" They went into an empty office. He pulled a legal document from his briefcase.

"Andrew McClaren named you in his will. He asked that I read this brief statement first."

Dearest Karen, you have been like a daughter to me. Your demonstration of caring and acts of kindness have touched my heart. No one cared for me as you have. You have been a light in my last days. Your obedient servant, Andrew McClaren.

"Now, let me finish reading the will. He finished with, 'All my property and one hundred fifty thousand dollars of savings, I bequeath to Karen S. Spanek.'"

Karen had to get her breath. The lawyer had her sign the document.

He finished by saying, "Everything will be transferred to you by next week."

She would tell Scott what had taken place. She went back to Scott's office and told him about the will.

In Stanton, Karen's home town, a different scene was taking place. It was hot on the plastic assembly line. The dirt, noise, and difficult assemblies wore on Ruth's mind. She wanted to go straight home after work. Gwendolyn Schwartz had been working with her all day.

The two women hadn't been talking much during their shift. Finally at four thirty, the whistle blew.

"Ruth, have you got a minute? Could I ask you to give me a ride home? My car is in the shop for the next two days."

Ruth had been feeling down lately. Something wasn't right at home. It appeared Ray, her husband, had been out of town on a number of extra trips. He had changed. But what was it? They were not close as they once were.

"Sure, Gwen, it won't take but a few minutes. Let me get my lunch bucket. You can give me a ride one day."

Ruth drove out of the parking lot, following Gwen's directions. Minutes later, they drove up to a house in need of repair. Gwen thanked her profusely then went inside.

Ruth turned on a through street. She saw a familiar pickup parked in the next block. It was Ray's truck. She parked behind two cars and waited to see what he was doing there. Ruth had a good view of the apartment building.

Thirty minutes later, Ray came out of an apartment followed by a tall, dark blonde woman.

The woman hugged and kissed Ray before he left driving away in his truck. Ruth drove home on a circuitous route. Ray was home when she arrived. She carried a bag of groceries into the kitchen.

So this is what is going on, Ruth thought. That explained a host of unanswered questions.

Ruth greeted Ray as she normally would. She was very mad and hurt at the way he was treating their marriage. She prepared supper just like always.

Ray left early Saturday morning, saying he had to work on his truck at a friend's house. After he left, Ruth went to a photography store. She purchased an expensive camera with a powerful zoom lens.

She practiced with her new camera. Her pictures were turning out very good quality. The following Wednesday morning, she asked Ray if he would be out of town that day or Thursday.

She noticed he had shaved and put on a new shirt. He answered her, "I'll be a little late. I have a run out of town in the afternoon today."

Ruth checked her camera equipment before going to work. She told Ed Barnes, her foreman, she would have to leave early at two thirty. A few minutes after two thirty, Ruth parked where her car was shaded behind some shrubbery.

She had a good view of the woman's apartment. She took several shots of the apartment. Promptly at three o'clock, Ray drove up, going to apartment 25.

He knocked on the door. Ruth took several shots of them standing in the doorway. They embraced and kissed. The woman's name was Jean Calmire, according to the city cross reference directory.

Two hours later, Ray came out of the apartment. Ruth stored her equipment in the trunk of her car. On the way home, she decided that going to a lawyer was the next step.

She felt sad and lonely as she drove home. So the stories that she had heard about Ray were true. She drove home slowly, with tears in her eyes. Friday, she went to a lawyer, taking the pictures of Ray with her. The lawyer would file the divorce papers she had signed. The pictures were good evidence of his infidelity. The lawyer assured her she would get half of his savings.

That evening, she went home to wait for Ray to show up. He came in, noting Ruth was sipping on a can of beer. He greeted her nonchalantly. Things were great for him. Two women—one, a homemaker and one, a lover.

"Sit down, Ray, and have a beer."

What was wrong? He questioned. No supper. What was on Suzie homemaker's mind? He got a beer from the refrigerator, then sat down across from her at the kitchen table. He was quiet. There were tears in her eyes as she spoke quietly and softly.

"Ray, I'm sorry, but I'm going to have to ask you to pack your things and leave. Pack as quickly as you can. Since we first were married, I have loved you. I thought we had something special. I've gone to bars with you, drank with you, kept the house clean, cooked, and never denied you anything. I know everything, and I hope you are happy with your new squeeze, Jean Calmire. Don't talk to me or touch me from now on. Now go!"

Ray was stunned as he sat there. He could see the tears in Ruth's eyes. She took only one sip from the beer can, pouring the rest in the sink. She sat back down, looking straight ahead as he got up from the table. He began to pack his clothes and things. Then he carried them out to his truck. He laid a key on the table and left.

The house was silent. Ruth laid her head in her arms, sobbing. She thought of the moment when Karen and Tiffany met her at work. She remembered the prophetic words that Tiffany had told her. Oh how she would like to change the outcome of that meeting.

It was really true. Ray Gould had to have been trying to molest her child. She was tired and upset. She took a hot bath and went into the kitchen to brew a pot of coffee and cook a solitary meal.

After dinner, she turned out the lights and went to bed. Her thoughts turned to her daughter. *Where can she be? What have I done?* She got up from the bed and picked up a large framed picture of Karen in her cap and gown.

She went back into the kitchen and held the picture in front of her. Ruth sat at the table and began to sob deeply. *She had only love for me, and I turned my baby out,* Ruth thought. *Tomorrow would be the first day of a better way of life,* she sobbed.

The night was a mixture of fear and nightmares. She awoke early. There was a new look in her eyes, a resolve. She threw her cigarettes in the trash. The next thing to go was the six pack of beer that had been sitting in the refrigerator. *I'll join Alcoholic Anonymous,* she vowed.

CHAPTER 19

In the morning, she would put on her best clothes and go to church. The craving for cigarettes and beer were strong, but she was determined. Sunday morning, Ruth went to Karen's church. Everyone welcomed her. She sat in a pew all alone. Tears flowed down her cheeks as she sat there. This was the first peace she had felt in many years.

"How long has it been since I have heard that lovely old hymn?" she asked herself.

Ruth was tired as her Stanton Junior College class began to close. The instructor was straightening her desk. The time was 9:30 p.m., and Ruth could feel the long day wearing on her.

Tuesday and Thursday classes won't kill me, she thought. This would be the second of two computer classes. They were adult evening classes at the college.

The first class was Introduction to Computers, and the second one was Windows. In the beginning, computers were Greek and difficult, but gradually, they became easy for her.

She was a good student in high school when she applied herself. Ruth made good grades, she recalled. She and Georgia Manning were the same age and taking the same courses. They would exchange confidences during classroom breaks.

Ruth was hesitant at first, but being alone now, she was more open. Ruth told Georgia everything.

"I was almost an alcoholic, Georgia. After my first husband died, I just seemed to lose it. So drinking was a crutch for me. In doing this, I have lost a beautiful daughter."

Georgia touched Ruth's hand. Ruth took an object out of her purse. It was a small aluminum cross.

"Georgia, I'm a recovering alcoholic. I attend meetings every week and will until I get stronger."

Ruth began by relating where she met Ray Gould, her second husband. How they would go out drinking, and that appeared to make drinking all right. She explained how at first she began sleeping with him.

"I suppose I was trying to find love and companionship in all the wrong places. I didn't have confidence or respect for myself."

Ruth was only repeating much of what she had told a counselor assigned by a local health organization.

"But you know, Georgia, I am going to make it. My daughter, Karen, is a wonderful Christian. Three months ago, I joined the church she attended. When I joined the church, I quit smoking and drinking cold turkey."

There were tears in Ruth's eyes as she related this to Georgia. Georgia handed her a Kleenex.

"Thank you for sharing all this with me, Ruth. I'm your friend, and I'll help you all I can."

"When I get all this behind me, I will locate Karen and ask her forgiveness."

The following months passed quickly for Ruth. She began to use makeup again. Following that, she acquired a nice wardrobe.

One evening after class, she received a telephone call from her instructor, Lisa Harold.

"Ruth, would you like a job with a huge credit card company?"

"You bet. Where do I go for the interview?"

Lisa described the company and the department in which she would work. "I've recommended you for this position, Ruth. You can do it!" Lisa exclaimed.

Monday morning, Ruth went to the Park credit card company personnel office. She gave the secretary her name. The manager Lisa had mentioned asked her to come into his office. What she saw was a well-dressed, manicured middle-aged woman.

"Ruth, you were well recommended to us by Lisa Harold. Matter of fact, you were the top student of your computer classes."

She began to explain the leadership they would need in their newly organized division. One hour later, Ruth returned to her car, walking on air. She bowed her head in prayer.

The work was like a tonic for her. No longer would she work at the plastic factory. Her life and personality just blossomed. With the higher income, she had her home remodeled and painted.

Gone was the old model automobile. Ruth now looked forward to Sunday and church. Her church was her best support through the previous rough times.

One Sunday, she went to the front of the church for special prayer. Friends surrounded her, praying with her. Next door, Molly could see the change in Ruth. Gone were the drinking and fighting. She remembered the months before the husband moved away.

Now something tremendous had taken hold of Ruth Spanek. Ruth had signed up for another class at Grafton. An idea popped into her head. She was still obsessed with finding Karen.

One Saturday, she was working outside on her flowerbeds. After an hour of hard work, she noticed Molly in her yard. Ruth went over to Molly's house, greeting her.

"Hi, Molly. How are you? It's been too long since we have visited."

Molly took a good look at her neighbor of many years and was astounded by the changes in Ruth. "Yes it has, Ruth. Your house looks so nice and pretty. Come and sit for a while in the porch swing."

Molly could see that Ruth wanted to confide in her. Ruth was quiet for just a moment, then began speaking.

"Oh, Molly, forgive me for telling you this. I have made such a mess of my life, but I am doing my best to try to turn it around. I've lost the most precious person in my life—Karen."

The tears ran down her face. She couldn't stop weeping. Deep sobs racked her body. Taking a handkerchief, she dried her eyes.

"Molly, I'll not stop looking until I find her and ask her forgiveness. I deserve everything that's happened to me since my husband died."

Ruth laid bare her very soul. She began by telling how she quit drinking and smoking and about her regular visits with Alcoholics Anonymous. Ruth explained how she had joined the church and attended regularly. She finished by telling Molly about her classes at Grafton Junior College and her new job. Molly knew of many of these changes in Ruth's life. Every Sunday without fail, Ruth would leave her home carrying a Bible.

Molly took her hand, consoling her. "Ruth, you know a wise man once said, 'It's not how you begin but how you finish.' You will find Karen, and she will forgive you."

"I'm beginning another evening course at Grafton. Perhaps I'll begin looking then. Good-bye, Molly, and thank you for being such a nice neighbor. I know you have always loved our Karen."

Molly took a deep breath. *Love would conquer after all,* she thought. It wouldn't be proper for her to tell Ruth about Karen. Ruth must make this quest herself.

Ruth arrived early for her class at Grafton. She was a few hours short of having an associate degree. The registrar's office was still open. The lady behind the counter asked Ruth if she could help her.

Ruth said, "I'm looking for Karen Spanek, a graduate of Grafton."

The lady said it would take a few minutes to get her file. Minute after anxious minute passed, and then she returned.

"All I have is an apartment address here in town. Karen was an A student and received a scholarship to go to Capitol City College."

"Thank you very much," Ruth replied.

It was too late after class to drive to Capitol City to check on Karen's address. She would look after work tomorrow.

The next day, Ruth's mind wasn't on her work. This was Thursday, and perhaps she would get lucky and find Karen today. She kept looking up at the clock in her office. At five o'clock, she left to check on the address given her at the registrar's office.

She drove slowly, looking for the street number. She parked in front of a two-story plain brick apartment building. She ran up the steps and into the hall.

The manager's office was on the first floor. After pushing on the doorbell, she stepped back, waiting. The door opened, and an older gray-haired woman in her sixties was standing there.

She was wearing a plain cotton dress. Her tennis shoes had seen better days.

"Can I help you? We are all full up right now."

"I am trying to locate my daughter, Karen Spanek. She would have been attending Grafton Junior College."

"Are you her mother, or are you from the welfare office?"

"I'm her mother."

Maude looked over the well-dressed woman standing before her. She noted the worried look on her face. "Well, she stayed here for about two years, and that was about two or three years ago."

"Would you possibly have her forwarding address?"

"Let me see if I can find that for you."

Maude left the doorway to go to a cluttered desk in a corner of the room. Papers were scattered all over it. Ruth watched her opening drawers. Finally, she pulled a dog-eared journal out of one drawer. Maude leafed through it, shaking her head.

"She worked for a television station. Karen was a beautiful girl, never any trouble. She and a friend rented 203 upstairs."

Ruth thanked her and returned to her car. Before getting into the car, she glanced at her watch. It would be too late to visit the television station. She would leave work early tomorrow. Now that she was a group manager, she had built up comp time.

Friday was a beautiful day, and Ruth was anxious for the day to end. Three o'clock found her driving to the television station. She went inside to the secretary's desk and asked to see the personnel manager.

The secretary led her to Marvin Decker's office. There was a man near her age sitting at the desk. She introduced herself to him. He noticed an attractive woman, dressed in fashionable clothing.

"How may I help you? I'm Marvin Decker. Your name sounds familiar."

"I'm trying to locate my daughter, Karen Spanek."

"Oh yes, I know who you mean. Karen had auburn hair, blue eyes, and was a beautiful girl, with personality plus. She did a very good job while working for us, but she left."

"Why did she leave, Mr. Decker?"

"Karen was driven toward an education. She had a scholarship at Capitol City University. We hated to see her leave as she was one of our best people."

He noticed the drawn look on Ruth's face. She dabbed at her eyes from time to time. "I believe she is working for a station in Capitol City."

Ruth rose to leave and extended her hand to Marvin Decker. He shook her hand. "I hope you find her, Mrs. Spanek." He could see the resemblance between mother and daughter. Karen had many of her mother's features.

Back in the car, Ruth decided to go home. She would pack a bag to stay overnight in Capitol City. After driving home, she quickly packed clothing for a weekend stay.

The late model Pontiac ate up the miles to Capitol City, and she arrived early in the afternoon. She went into a store and asked for a phone book and purchased a map of the city. She located the television station and went inside. Ruth got the attention of one of the office workers there. The young woman asked Ruth if she could help her.

"Does Karen Spanek work here?"

"You must mean Karen Chapin. She got married not too long ago."

"Do you have her last known address? I'm her mother, and I'm trying to locate her."

"I sure do. Let me go in the office and get it for you." Ruth felt rather faint as she waited.

"Will you want the phone number also? Are you all right, ma'am? Can I get you a glass of water?"

The girl noticed the worried look on Ruth's face, handing her the address written on a slip of paper. Ruth asked the young woman how to go to the address and wrote the instructions down.

Her heart fluttered as she returned to her car. She was undecided as to what to do, and it was getting late. Finally, she resolved to go ahead. Driving carefully, she was soon in an older part of town.

Stately, older well-kept houses lined a wide boulevard. Such beautiful old houses with well-manicured lawns.

Looking ahead, she saw a two-story brick house on the right hand side of the street. There was a three-car garage with an attached apartment. The windows were dressed with white shutters. The backyard was surrounded with a black wrought iron fence. It had many large shade trees and a lovely lawn.

The metal fence had been installed many years ago. Such a beautiful old house. There was someone home. Ruth could hear children playing inside as she drove up. This had to be the correct address, all the numbers matched.

The scene before her was a quiet one, giving her a sense of peace. She said a silent prayer as she prepared to go to the door. She looked at her face in the mirror. She began walking toward the door.

Scott was playing with Paige and Tyler, while Karen was preparing an evening meal. They were dining later than usual. He glanced out the window. Someone in a late model Pontiac had parked in front of the house.

An attractive lady was getting out. She was dressed in a fashionable pants suit. Her hair was an auburn color, similar to Karen's. She somehow looked familiar. But who?

She came up on the porch and rang the doorbell. Scott went to answer the door, followed by the children.

He said, "May I help you?"

"I'm looking for Karen Spanek."

"That would be my wife, Karen. Her maiden name was Spanek."

Ruth's eyes glistened upon seeing two little blonde, blue-eyed children holding to their father's leg. The young man at the door was big, with sandy hair. He was built like a football player, well over six feet tall.

"Oh, forgive my manners. Won't you step inside?"

She saw his huge hands lovingly guide the children away from the door. She could see the love he had for them. Just then, a voice came from the back of the house. "Who it is, Scott?"

Karen had been busy preparing their evening meal when the doorbell rang. She heard Scott talking to someone, and she was curious.

Then Scott called to her, "Honey, can you come here?"

Ruth knew it was Karen when she heard her voice. She felt fear clutching at her heart. What could she say to her beloved daughter whom she had hurt? Those split moments caused her to feel unfit, not knowing what to do or say. Could her daughter ever forgive her?

Karen turned the heat on the stove down to low, before going into the front room. Ruth heard Karen coming into the room. There she was, her daughter Karen. She was a grown woman standing there. She kept her eyes on Karen, unable to speak.

Karen was stunned. She saw a well-dressed woman. Her hair was well-styled, and she didn't look anything like the mother she once knew.

Karen spoke softly, bewildered. Who was this person? "Are you my mother?"

Ruth could no longer stand. She began to sob uncontrollably while looking at Karen. She sat down on a nearby couch, taking a handkerchief from her purse.

"Yes, I am, sweetheart. Can you ever forgive me for what I've done?"

CHAPTER 20

Karen and Scott sat down across from Ruth. The children stood near their parents.

"She cry, Mama," one said.

Karen could see the tremendous changes that had taken place in her mother. What made her mother change and turn her life around?

Karen began to weep while holding on to Scott's hand. Ruth laid her head down on the arm of the couch. She continued to weep. Karen was in awe at how her mother was dressed and the change in her.

"What have I done? I came to realize how much you mean to me." Ruth was feeling lonelier than ever at that moment. Would she have to leave, not knowing forgiveness?

Karen rose slowly, going over to sit behind her mother. Ruth was unaware that Karen had sat down behind her. She felt a hand touch her shoulder. She turned, and there was her daughter, smiling with tears in her eyes.

"Mother, you have no idea how long I've waited for you to love me."

"Oh, Karen, say that you will forgive me. I love you."

The mother and daughter were crying together, in each other's arms.

"I do, Mother, and I'm happy we are together again forever."

Between sobs, Karen said, "Mother I want you to meet my husband, Scott Chapin."

Ruth rose to hug Scott. Then she hugged Karen and kissed her on the cheek. Scott offered both the women tissues.

"Oh, I almost forgot about supper. It might burn." Karen dashed into the kitchen. Supper was ready to serve. "Mother, you are so different. You look so sophisticated and beautiful. Just look at that hair and clothes, Scott. Mama, are you hungry? We want you to eat with us."

"I am hungry. I've been looking for you, darling, forgetting to eat." Ruth looked at the two children sitting at the table. "Who are these two little angels, Scott?"

Scott introduced Paige and Tyler to their new grandmother, Ruth. Karen set another plate for Ruth. They all took their seats. Ruth asked to say grace, breaking down once. They enjoyed the delicious food and each other's company.

The meal over, the mother and daughter cleaned up the kitchen together. They stopped twice to hug each other once again while they cleaned.

When the kitchen was cleaned, Karen led Ruth back into the living room. Scott told them to visit while he bathed the children for bedtime.

"What a neat man Scott is. You two seem to be so happy."

The mother and daughter were chatting like magpies when Scott led the children back into the room. They were dressed for bed. The time was *8:45* p.m. Both children climbed up onto Karen's lap.

She talked to them. Paige let Ruth hold her, "It's time to go to bed, kids," Karen stated. Each parent carried a child. They started to go upstairs to their bedroom.

"May I go with you and watch you tuck them in?" Ruth asked.

"Grandmothers are supposed to help tuck kids in, Mother."

Ruth followed them into the bedroom. It was decorated with a pretty Mother Goose theme. There were twin beds for the children. Scott and Karen kissed each child. Ruth, unable to resist, kissed them on the cheek.

"Good night, sweet dreams, little angels," Ruth said.

"I wanted to wait until the children were in bed before we visited," Karen said as they returned to the living room. They sat down near each other. Ruth began her story first. She related how Ray Gould began drinking heavily, how he ran around on her, and how they finally split up getting a divorce.

"It was then that I realized that I had hit bottom, Karen. I took a good look at my life. Then I decided to do something about it. First, I was going to change my lifestyle, then find my daughter. I began taking evening classes at Grafton. I found I was good with computers. Then joined Alcoholics Anonymous and quit smoking. Now I have a very good job, and I feel like a whole new person.

"Thank you, Scott and Karen, for listening. I love you both very much. How lucky I am to be here with my family now. Karen, you will be happy to know that I joined your church and attend regularly. I got a second chance. How many get that anyway?"

What Karen saw was an entirely different mother than the one she had left. She began her story with sharing an apartment with Tiffany and the long hours working and studying.

She then related to Ruth the details of her rape, what followed after Paige's birth, and the move to Capitol City. Karen told her about Andrew's sickness and death. She mentioned the will Andrew left.

"But, Mother, I saved the best for last." Karen moved to Scott's side, taking his hand in hers. "I met the most wonderful man in the world." She looked directly into Scott's eyes. "We have so much in common and a child apiece. This man knows all about me. We have no secrets between us. He went to church with me. We didn't want to live without each other, so here we are. He has such wonderful parents." She kissed Scott's cheek. He hugged her back.

It was getting late, and Ruth picked up her purse to leave.

"Mother, where are you going?"

"I packed an overnight bag to stay in the city looking for you. I'll find some place to stay overnight."

"Mama, you are staying here with us in this big old house. We have two more bedrooms just waiting for guests. You don't want me to have Scott carry you upstairs, do you?" She laughed. "He could do it," Karen said.

"Scott, let me hug you before I go to bed. Can you put up with a new mother-in-law?"

"You bet!" Then he hugged Ruth.

He got her car keys and brought her bag inside and carried it upstairs. All three trooped upstairs to a large comfortable room. The view was a good one of the entire city. They both hugged her, saying good night. Ruth hesitated while looking out the window.

"Mother, we want you to get used to being here with us. Now we have you forever. In the morning, we will catch up with all our visiting.

"Sweet dreams."

Scott left the two women alone. He felt a peace as he went downstairs. This chapter of Karen's life was complete now that she had her mother back.

Ruth was in bed now. The night sounds were so peaceful. Then she said a short prayer before closing her eyes. A thought clouded her mind. From now on, I'll go Karen's way.

Aaron H. Foster began writing after retiring. He took three writing courses at a local college. God gave him much imagination. He has since written three 50,000 word novels and ninety short stories. He is a published author. He resides in Tulsa, Oklahoma.

CPSIA information can be obtained
at www.ICGtesting.com
Printed in the USA
LVHW091421110319
610216LV00001B/64/P